Sunset Island

CHERIE BENNETT

SPLASH™

A BERKLEY / SPLASH BOOK

SUNSET ISLAND is an original publication
of The Berkley Publishing Group.
This work has never appeared before in book form.

A Berkley Book / published by arrangement with
General Licensing Company, Inc.

PRINTING HISTORY
Berkley edition / June 1991

A GLC BOOK

Splash is a trademark of General Licensing Company, Inc.

ISBN: 0-425-12969-1

A BERKLEY BOOK ® TM 757,375
Berkley Books are published by The Berkley Publishing Group,
200 Madison Avenue, New York, New York 10016.
The name "BERKLEY" and the "B" logo
are trademarks belonging to Berkley Publishing Corporation.

PRINTED IN THE UNITED STATES OF AMERICA

10 9 8 7 6 5 4 3 2 1

"Hey, I believe we create our own destiny," Kurt said seriously.

"If you want it, you should go for it."

Emma smiled into the darkness. "I'll keep that in mind." Something in the sky caught her eye. "Look! A shooting star!"

"Make a wish!" Kurt ordered.

Emma closed her eyes. I wish he would kiss me, she thought. When she opened her eyes Kurt was staring at her. She could just barely make out his face in the starlight.

"What did you wish for?" he asked softly.

"I thought I wasn't supposed to tell," Emma whispered.

"Ah, an honorable woman," Kurt said. "My favorite kind."

He gently stroked her hair. Then he drew her face to his, and kissed her lightly. Pulling back from her, he stared at her face a moment, then he kissed her again. Only this time his arms went gently around her, and she gave herself up completely to the incredible, fabulous feeling of kissing him back.

Well, well, Emma thought. I guess wishes on shooting stars really can come true.

And she kissed him again.

Coming soon
in the SUNSET ISLAND
series

Sunset Kiss
Sunset Dreams
Sunset Farewell

This book is for Jeff

ONE

Emma stood at the doorway of the ballroom at the Marriott hotel in New York City, underneath the huge banner that read INTERNATIONAL AU PAIR CONVENTION. She looked around uncertainly at the throngs of people milling through the ballroom, searching for a friendly face.

Eighteen-year-olds from all over the world had come to this convention, in the hopes of being hired as au pairs. Some were just looking for a great summer job before college. Some hoped to be hired for an entire year. But all of them were counting on landing a job in some choice location.

Emma had to smile, thinking about it. Six months ago she hadn't even known what an au pair was. Then the Powells, friends of her parents, hired an eighteen-year-old French girl through the International Au Pair Society to care for their children for a year. Monique lived in their home and sort of became a part of their family. In addition to room and board, she also received a small salary. The more Emma thought about it, the more she thought that this would be the perfect summer job for her.

Not that her parents agreed, of course. In fact,

they had been horrified. Why on earth should Emma work at all? It wasn't as if she needed the money, they added reasonably. But how could Emma explain to her extremely rich, extremely self-satisfied parents that she didn't want the job for the money? She wanted it to get away from her extremely rich, extremely self-satisfied parents.

Sometimes Emma thought she would suffocate, just drown within the narrow confines of her parents' life-style. It often seemed that every minute of her life had been prearranged, from the right Swiss boarding schools to the right Waspy, old-money friends. In the fall, her parents expected Emma to go to Ballantrae College, which in her opinion was an elitist, all-women finishing school. It was also the college that her mother and her mother's mother had attended. Emma would concentrate on French, an "appropriate" major for a rich girl. But really, Emma didn't want to go to Ballantrae. She didn't want to study French. And she didn't want to go along with all the "shoulds" that had been dictated to her all of her life.

The plan had formed slowly in her mind, gathering steam over the last few months. She would go to the International Au Pair Convention in New York in April. She knew she could stay at her Aunt Liz's loft in SoHo during the convention. She'd go through the training and the lectures and the interviews, and at the end of the convention she'd be hired as an au pair for some nice family at some fabulous location. Someplace where no one knew she was a Cresswell of *the* Boston Cresswells. Someplace where she could be just like everyone else.

"Emma! Emma! Over here!"

Emma was startled back to the present. She looked through the crowd in the direction of the voice that was calling her. Over the tops of the heads of a couple of hundred girls and a handful of guys, Emma spied the wild red curls and waving arms of Samantha Bridges. Emma had sat next to Sam at the very first lecture of the convention two days earlier, and they had gotten to be friends. Sam had made the getting-to-know-each-other process easy. She was like that—and unlike anyone else Emma had ever known. Emma waved back gratefully and made her way toward Sam.

"Here, have some coffee," Sam said, handing Emma a paper cup from the long buffet table set up behind her. "What a scene, huh?"

"Unbelievable," Emma agreed, as someone bumped her from behind to get to the breakfast buffet.

Sam helped steady Emma and caught a good look at Emma's outfit.

"Wow, some rags you got on," Sam said, looking over Emma's perfect, pleated gray flannel pants and cream-colored blazer. "Hey, I recognize that blazer! I saw it in last month's *Town and Country*!" Sam exclaimed. "In fact, I saw the

3

whole outfit. It's an Elan original, right? Jeez, that must have cost a mint!"

The last thing Emma wanted Sam to know was how rich she was.

"Oh, um, this?" Emma stammered. "It's, uh . . ."

"Oh, there's Carrie, over by the door," Sam interrupted. "Hey, Carrie!" she called, waving madly in Carrie's direction.

Emma waved too, although the ladylike wave of five feet five Emma could not be seen nearly as well as the manic wave of five feet ten Sam. Emma was just thankful Sam was distracted from examining her outfit.

"Do you know Carrie's going to Yale in the fall? Yale!" Sam whispered to Emma.

"Really?" Emma said. "I'm impressed."

"Me, too!" Sam agreed. "She told me yesterday. She got something impossible like sixteen hundred on her SATs. I don't think she wants it to get around that she's such a brain, though," Sam added. "God, my stomach is grumbling. Do they call doughnuts and rolls breakfast?"

Emma laughed and shook her head. Sam was so excited and enthusiastic about everything. She also skipped maddeningly from one topic to another.

Sam grabbed a roll from the table as Emma watched Carrie work her way through the crowd. Emma and Sam had met Carrie the day before when the three of them had been teamed up at a workshop called "Child Care and Problem Solv-

4

ing." Each team had been given a different theoretical problem. Emma, Carrie, and Sam's problem had been: "You are caring for a thirteen-year-old girl who wants to have a party at her house while her parents are out of town. What do you do?" Emma, who felt the least sure of herself regarding caring for kids, said tentatively that she would just tell the girl no. Practical Carrie agreed, but added that she would explain why and would suggest an alternative, such as planning a party that the girl could give once her parents returned. Sam said she would tell the girl she could give the party, but only if she also invited the cutest older brothers of all of her thirteen-year-old friends. Fortunately the teacher had a sense of humor.

"Whew! What a madhouse!" Carrie exclaimed when she finally made it over to Emma and Sam.

"Hey, cute outfit!" Sam said, eyeing Carrie's oversized blue blazer and blue stirrup pants. "Conservative, but cute."

"I really didn't know what to wear," Carrie confided. "You guys look great," she added. "That jacket is beautiful, Emma."

Emma smiled and winced inside. Oh no, back to her clothes again. How could she have been so stupid as to wear such expensive designer clothes? Because that was all she owned, was the obvious answer.

"'Beautiful' is an understatement," Sam burst out. "I'd kill my little sister for a blazer like that. Of course, I'd kill my little sister, anyway. You

5

know, I think Princess Caroline wore that blazer on 'Lifestyles of the Rich and Famous,'" she added.

Carrie turned to Sam. "You actually watch 'Lifestyles of the Rich and Famous'?"

"I inhale 'Lifestyles of the Rich and Famous'," Sam answered seriously. "Although it looks like Emma is a lot closer to getting on that show than I am."

"Oh sure," Emma managed. "Actually, this outfit belongs to my Aunt Liz. I'm staying with her for the weekend."

"Nice aunt," Carrie said.

"*Rich* aunt," Sam added.

"Yeah, she, um, invested in the stock market," Emma improvised. "She's got great taste. I guess I just wanted to make a good impression," Emma added.

"Yeah, well, it makes a great impression all right," Sam said. "I probably look totally shabby next to you, and no one will hire me."

Sam had on a full black cotton skirt that fell just above the knee, a white cotton shirt with black hearts on it, and red cowboy boots. Her long red curls were held back with a black velvet ribbon, but tendrils escaped around her pretty, flushed face. Her blue eyes were rimmed with carefully smudged eyeliner, and her full lips were painted a deep, matte red.

Carrie laughed, looking Sam over. "Give me a break. You look spectacular. I bet you look spectacular when you wake up in the morning."

"Not me," Sam said to Carrie. "Now Emma here, on the other hand, really is the perfect type." Sam turned to Emma. "You've got that blond ice princess, born-to-money kind of look. Very Grace Kelly."

Emma laughed uncomfortably. "I wish," she said.

"Me, too," said Carrie.

"You mean you wish you had the look or you wish you had the money?" Sam asked her.

"Both!" Carrie said. "If I hear just once more in my life that I look like the girl next door, I'm going to throw up."

Sam reached behind her and snatched a doughnut off the buffet table. "Actually, you're extremely cute," Sam said, chewing and studying Carrie thoughtfully. "You've got great, glossy hair, and a seriously curvy figure hiding somewhere under that outfit." Sam took a sip of her coffee. "Of course, there is hardly a girl on the planet who can't be helped by a fashion makeover and some well-applied cosmetics."

Carrie laughed and made a face. "Thanks for the grooming tip, but I hate makeup. I never wear it."

"Never say never!" Sam sang out. "Hopefully we'll end up in the same place, and I'll have the whole summer to work on you."

The three girls had discussed it the evening before, looking over the various locations they might choose. They all wanted to be in a resort community and not in a city. They all wanted to go someplace where there would be a lot of kids their age. They had decided their first choice would be Sunset Island.

Emma thought dreamily about how fabulous the island sounded. Sunset Island was described in their au pair book as "a small resort island off the coast of Maine. In the summertime, the population of Sunset Island swells to 50,000 people, who take advantage of all this upscale resort community has to offer. Sunset Island has won awards for everything from the architecture of its summer homes to the breathtaking beauty of its sandy beaches nestled into a craggy shoreline."

"Are you nervous about the interviews?" Sam asked Emma.

Emma was startled back from her vision of miles of gorgeous beach filled with miles of gorgeous guys, none of whom would have a clue as to who she was.

"Pardon me?" Emma said.

"I said today's the big day, but you were a million miles a way," Sam told Emma. "And I asked you if you were nervous about it. I am."

Emma smiled ruefully. "Yeah, I guess I am, too."

"I mean, what if no one hires me?" Sam continued. "Or what if I only get an offer from someplace gruesome—like Kansas."

Emma had to laugh. Sam thought working in Kansas would be gruesome because that's where she had lived all her life. It was the last place on earth she wanted to spend the summer.

"Ladies and gentlemen, may I have your attention?" a voice boomed from the podium microphone. It was Ms. Van Cleef, the president of the International Au Pair Society. A hush fell over the room as everyone turned to listen to her announcement.

"As you all know, today is the big day," Ms. Van Cleef continued. "When you enter the conference room, you'll find tables have been set up for each employment location that was described in your au pair books. You've all received a computer list showing your first, second, and third choice of location. We only gave second choices when a location was simply overloaded as a first choice," she explained.

Emma, Sam, and Carrie looked at their sheets and grinned. They'd really lucked out—all getting their first choice.

"Please proceed to the table with the sign marked with the name of your area," Ms. Van Cleef went on. "Once you are all settled, we'll invite your prospective employers in to interview you. I wish you all the best of luck and a wonderful au pair experience," she concluded.

There was polite applause as the double doors opened into the conference room. The crowd streamed through the doors and headed for their proper table.

"It's over there!" Sam called, spying the large Sunset Island sign. She led her friends toward

9

the long table. Four chairs were set up behind the table for the au pairs, with lots of chairs set up for the prospective employers on the opposite side.

"I wonder who the fourth au pair is," Carrie asked, eyeing the empty seat.

She didn't have to wait long to find out. A black-haired beauty with startling light blue eyes and a gorgeous, golden tan rushed over to the table.

"Not Lorell," Sam groaned under her breath. "Anyone but Lorell."

Lorell Courtland hailed from Atlanta, Georgia, and was as wealthy as she was obnoxious. Lorell had been in Sam's first "get acquainted" group. As Lorell had let everyone in the group know, she had recently made her debut at the Beaux Arts Ball in Atlanta, and she had flown in to New York for the convention in her daddy's private jet. When Sam had finally asked her why she was bothering to work for the summer, Lorell just laughed and said that her daddy thought it would "build her character." Lorell rolled her eyes heavenward when she said this, as if the idea was just too droll. Sam privately doubted that Lorell had any character to build.

"Hey, y'all!" Lorell trilled. "Why Sammi, how utterly fantastic that we should be goin' to the same place!" Lorell sat down next to Carrie and pushed her sleek black hair behind one diamond-studded ear.

"Hi, Lorell," Sam answered her. "Do you guys

know each other?" she asked Emma and Carrie. They shook their heads no, so Sam introduced them to Lorell.

Lorell gave them her most winning smile. "I'm so pleased to meet you," she purred.

"Where did you get such a terrific tan in April?" Carrie asked Lorell.

"Oh, we have a tanning salon in the gym on our estate," Lorell explained.

"We do, too," Sam said in a total deadpan, "but I prefer the pale look."

Lorell laughed as if this was just the funniest thing she had ever heard. She knew Sam lived in the tiny town of Junction, Kansas, and she knew Sam's family was totally middle class. "Oh, Sammi, you are just hilarious!"

Carrie looked at Sam. "Sammi?"

Lorell stared appraisingly at Emma's outfit and raised her eyebrows. "Lovely ensemble," she said. "And the watch is a Cartier, isn't it?"

Emma blushed and tried to look nonchalant. "It was a graduation present," she said smoothly.

"Isn't that sweet," Lorell said.

Sam sighed. "My parents gave me a trip to Washington, D.C., as a graduation present. I was supposed to watch democracy in action. Instead, a congressman tried to pick me up."

"They're going to let the vultures in any minute," Lorell remarked. "I plan to choose a family with only one child, and that child better be old enough to take care of his- or herself!"

"Hey, do I still have any lipstick on or did I eat

11

it all off?" Sam asked nervously. She rummaged through her purse for a mirror.

"It's still on," Carrie assured her.

"Darn, I forgot my compact," Sam said.

"Here, I've got a mirror," Emma said, reaching into her bag for her compact. She found it and handed it to Sam.

"I suppose that was a graduation gift, too?" Lorell asked coolly. Too late Emma realized what she had done. Her compact was sterling silver and engraved with her initials.

Sam checked her lipstick and then snapped the compact shut for a better look. "Wow, Emma, this is gorgeous! What are you, some kind of secret baroness or something?"

Emma reached for her compact and shoved it back into her purse. "It's my aunt's," Emma said quickly. "Her name is Elizabeth. We have the same initials."

Lorell stared intently at Emma. Emma could feel her heart racing. She was going to have to watch out for Lorell, that was for sure.

"I've got to meet this aunt!" Sam said, oblivious of the look that had passed between Emma and Lorell. "Do you think she might want to adopt me?"

"Here they come!" Carrie called out, as the doors opened and masses of people poured into the conference room.

Soon all four girls were immersed in interviews. After a while some other au pairs, who'd listed Sunset Island as their second choice, joined the table. In case a prospective employer wasn't happy with Emma, Carrie, Sam, or Lorell, they could choose one of the other applicants.

Two hours later, it was all over and the last few interviewers straggled out of the conference room.

"God, that was worse than college interviews," Carrie said, laying her head on the table.

"The people were nice, though, didn't you think?" Emma asked. "Especially the Hewitts."

Jane and Jeff Hewitt had been the first people to interview Emma, and she had liked them right away. They really put her at ease, telling her about themselves and their family before asking her any questions. Both Jane and Jeff were lawyers and they had three kids. They lived in Bangor during the year and had a summer house on Sunset Island.

"Forget nice," Sam said. "Did you see how cute Jeff Hewitt is?"

Carrie looked horrified. "He must be at least thirty-five years old!"

"So what's that, geriatric?" Sam asked. "I loved the way his biceps bulged out of his tennis shirt. Very hot."

"What about that mysterious Mr. Rudolph," said Lorell. "He told me he was the general manager for some people named Templeton."

"Why would someone send an employee to interview the person who's going to take care of their kids?" Carrie wondered. "You'd think they'd be a little more concerned than that."

"Because they're megarich, of course," Lorell

said. "I'm going to have to ask Daddy if he knows the Templetons. He will if they're on the Hammersley list."

"What's the Hammersley list?" Carrie asked.

"It lists the four hundred richest families in America," Lorell told her.

"And I suppose your family is on it," Sam said.

"Well, aren't you sweet to assume that," Lorell cooed. "And, of course, you're right. The Courtlands have been on it ever since it was first published, which was just eons ago." Lorell turned to Emma. "What's your last name again, Emma?" she asked innocently.

Emma knew about that list. In fact, her family was somewhere up in the top hundred names on it.

"Cresswell," Emma said softly.

"Cresswell?" Lorell echoed. "That sounds so familiar. Where did y'all say you were from?"

"I didn't, but I'm from Boston," Emma said evenly.

"Cresswells from Boston," Lorell mused. "Hmmm . . ."

Emma knew she was in hot water. Lorell was the kind of snob that Emma had been around all her life. She probably had the Hammersley list memorized.

"Oh, you must be thinking of the other Cresswells," Emma said with a laugh. "I read about them in the society pages all the time. I wish they were at least distant cousins or something! So,

14

when do we find out if we got hired?" Emma said, changing the subject as quickly as possible.

"The booklet said we can expect a call from the placement committee within the next week," Carrie said. "I hope we all got jobs."

"We did," Sam said. "I'm sure of it."

The other girls looked at her.

"It's called the power of positive thinking," Sam said, standing up to stretch.

Emma stood up, too. "I'm starving," she said. "I guess I was too nervous to eat breakfast."

"Hey, let's go out, have lunch, and celebrate," Sam suggested.

"I'd love to," Lorell purred, "but I made an appointment for a facial." Lorell adjusted the perfect neckline of her pink cashmere sweater with one French-manicured finger. "Y'all have a fun time, and I just know we're goin' to become great friends this summer. I've got to run. Bye now!" Emma, Sam, and Carrie stared after her.

"I hope having money doesn't automatically make a person obnoxious," Sam said, shaking her head, "since I plan to become extremely rich one of these days."

The three girls walked slowly toward the door of the conference room.

"I think maybe she's just really insecure or something," Carrie said. "I mean, every other word out of her mouth is about how rich she is."

"Where should we eat?" Emma asked when they got outside. She was sick of thinking and talking about money.

"There's a coffee shop across the street," Sam said, pointing to a sign that read ACROPOLIS DINER.

The girls found an empty booth inside and studied the menus. When they were ready to order, Emma went first.

"I'll have a spinach salad and coffee," she said.

"I'll have the same," Carrie said with a sigh.

"I'll have a salad, a bacon cheeseburger, fries *and* onion rings," Sam said. "Oh, and a chocolate milkshake," she added. Her friends stared at her. "What?" she asked innocently. "I'm hungry!"

Emma and Carrie broke up and then Sam did, too.

"There is no justice in the world!" Carrie said. "You eat like a pig and you look like a model!"

Sam went into some story about how it hadn't been so much fun being five ten at the age of twelve, and how her seventh-grade class had nicknamed her the Stork, but Emma was only half-listening. She was thinking about how nice Sam and Carrie were. It was going to be so great, spending the summer with them. Emma crossed her fingers superstitiously under the table. If she could only please, please, get a job offer on Sunset Island, she might just have the very best summer of her life.

TWO

Emma hugged herself as she stared into the mirror over her vanity table. "Emma Cresswell," she whispered to herself, "in just a few hours you will be on beautiful, romantic Sunset Island." Just hearing the name sent shivers down her spine.

She'd been hired by Jane and Jeff Hewitt as their au pair. Out of all the people who had interviewed Emma, the Hewitts had been her absolute favorites. They seemed so kind, so down-to-earth and unpretentious. *All qualities lacking in my family*, Emma had thought ruefully.

As soon as she'd found out, Emma had run downstairs to tell her mother, but her mother, as usual, wasn't home. Then she phoned Sam and Carrie, hoping that they'd heard, too. And they had! All three girls would be together for the summer on Sunset Island. Emma had never been so excited about anything in her life.

Now the day to leave had finally arrived. Emma studied her reflection in the mirror, wondering if she looked okay. She brushed a little more blush over her cheeks, and tucked her

17

white oxford shirt into her khaki pants. This outfit she had truly borrowed from her Aunt Liz. She wanted to make a good impression, but she also wanted to make the right impression. And the right impression meant looking like everyone else.

She had planned it all very carefully. Out went the sterling silver initialed compact, the two-karat diamond-stud earrings, the Cartier watch, and the perfect pearls. Into the suitcase went her only pair of jeans, a leotard she used to work out in, her oldest bathing suit, and two T-shirts (also borrowed from Aunt Liz).

Aunt Liz was Emma's best friend and closest confidante. She was the younger sister of Emma's mother, definitely the black sheep of the family. In her early thirties, single, and living in a loft in New York City, Liz was the antithesis of Emma's mother. Emma's mother was utterly self-centered and completely useless—unless you counted her self-proclaimed vocation as a "patroness of the arts." Liz had a really important job as director of the National Environmental Health Organization.

Emma smiled, remembering what had happened when she explained her wardrobe dilemma to her aunt. Liz had understood right away.

"Well, of course you're going to stick out like a sore thumb in that designer stuff. How about we go shopping?" she suggested. "It'll be fun. All the best places for cheap, funky clothes are right here in SoHo."

Emma smiled gratefully at her aunt. "I was thinking, I don't know, maybe I should buy my clothes when I get there. What do you think?"

Liz had hugged Emma. "I think that's a great idea. Then you'll know exactly the right things to get. I'm so proud of you for taking this job, Emma."

Liz had also given Emma the best present, a tapestry-covered journal and a beautiful calligraphy pen.

"This is an important summer for you, Emma," Liz had said. "Your life is going through a lot of changes. I thought you might like to keep a journal, you know, to record your thoughts and feelings. I know my own journal has helped me get through some of the rougher times in my life."

Emma looked lovingly at the exquisite book, which now sat on top of her suitcase. For some reason it made her feel more confident, just knowing it was there.

Emma still stared at her face in the mirror, wondering how she looked to her new friends. She remembered Sam calling her "the perfect type," and she made a face at her reflection. Emma had a sudden urge to rat up her hair, pile on makeup, and chew gum with her mouth open. Oh, right, I'm really daring, Emma thought to herself with disgust. My idea of being wild is chewing gum with my mouth open. She laughed and stuck her tongue out at herself, then brushed her hair into its usual sleek perfection.

Finally ready to go, Emma sat on her bed to reread Carrie's latest letter. Ever since Emma had called Carrie and Sam to find out if they'd gotten jobs on Sunset Island, they had all been writing to each other. Well, actually Carrie and Emma had been writing. Emma had received one letter from Sam scribbled hastily on the back of a cocktail napkin from some club called Dangerous in Manhattan. Manhattan, Kansas. Sam said she was out at that very moment with two college guys and couldn't decide which one she liked better. She said she was counting the days until they'd all meet at Sunset Island. She signed the cocktail napkin with a lip print, then added a P.S.: "Don't expect any more letters, I'm a crummy correspondent."

Carrie, on the other hand, had proved to be an excellent pen pal. This was the fifth letter Emma had received from her, and Emma had written four back to Carrie.

It's after midnight, (Carrie's letter read), *and I'm dashing this off to you before I fall on my face. So much has happened since my last letter. Remember the New Jersey State Teen Photographer's Contest I told you I was entering? I had taken these great photos of me and my boyfriend, Josh, all dressed up to go to the prom. (It's not hard to do—you just use a timer on the camera.) I don't know, maybe it was just that I had spent so many years thinking about my* senior prom, but somehow everything seemed kind of flat. Have you ever felt that way? I felt really sad and I couldn't figure out why. It's not like I'm not thrilled to be getting out of high school, because I am. Anyway, Josh got bummed out that I was so bummed out, so that bummed me out even more. We started talking about the fall, about how I'll be at Yale and he'll be at Stanford, and how it's so hard to have a long-distance relationship. So Josh says he thinks we should be engaged to be engaged. I just looked at him. I'm thinking I'm only seventeen years old! I don't want to be engaged to be engaged! Then I hear myself tell him that maybe we should break up instead. I couldn't believe I was saying it! I love Josh! I've loved Josh since the eighth grade! So we had this big fight, and I cried all my mascara off (Sam would be happy to know I was wearing some makeup for once) and got big mascara blotches all over my dress. It was the worst night of my life. When I got home I set up the timer on my camera and took a picture of myself, sitting on the bed looking like a total wreck. I have absolutely no idea why I did that. And I have absolutely no idea why I entered that picture in the contest instead of the ones of me and Josh looking so happy. But . . . I ended up placing second in the contest! So now I have a red ribbon and no boyfriend.

21

"Emma, Lawrence is ready to drive you to the airport."

The voice of Mrs. James, the Cresswell's housekeeper (or household manager, as she preferred to be called, since it was her job to manage household staff), startled Emma.

"I'll be right down," Emma said, folding Carrie's letter and putting it in her pocket.

Emma took a final look at herself in the mirror before heading downstairs to say good-bye to her mother. Her mother was on the phone, and she gave a little wave at Emma and held up one finger while she finished her conversation.

"Yes . . . yes, of course, darling, of course I'll miss you," Emma's mother purred breathily into the phone.

Emma turned away from her mother and made a face. She wished she could tell her mother that a breathy, girlish voice was not exactly sexy coming from a forty-eight-year-old woman.

". . . Oh Austin, you know I'm trying as hard as I can," Emma's mother continued into the phone. "But Brent expects me to give him the moon with a fence around it in the settlement. It's just too ludicrous!"

Emma winced. She hated overhearing these conversations of her mother's, where she bitched and moaned about the complications of divorcing Emma's father. The divorce proceedings had been going on for over a year. Neither her father nor her mother had been willing to give an inch. Sometimes she felt a little sorry for her father. It was, after all, her mother who was having the affair with twenty-five-year-old artist Austin Payne. It was her mother who—much to Emma's embarrassment—actually planned to marry this jerk when her divorce was final.

"Yes, Austin, my love . . . ," Emma's mother purred.

Oh God. Emma just wanted to put her hands over her ears and block it all out.

"Mother, I've got to go," was all she said.

Katerina Cresswell (whose second sentence to anyone was invariably "Please call me Kat"), held up one finger again, and Emma sighed with impatience.

"Austin, darling, I've got to run. Emma's leaving on her little trip and I want to say good-bye. I'll call you later. Ciao, darling." Kat made kissing noises into the phone, then hung up. "So, let me look at you, sweetheart," Kat said to Emma, and crossed to her with her arms out wide. She kissed the air in the vicinity of Emma's right cheek, then in the vicinity of her left cheek.

"I don't recognize that outfit," Kat said, frowning at Emma.

"Aunt Liz gave it to me," Emma said.

"How nice," said Kat coolly, conveying in her tone of voice that of course it really wasn't nice at all.

"What am I supposed to do, show up in a Paris original?" Emma asked her mother defensively. "I'm going there to work, in case you've forgotten."

Kat laughed gaily. "Who would believe I have a daughter old enough to work!"

"I am old enough," Emma said. "I want this job. A lot."

Kat sighed. "So you've said. Sometimes your choices are simply beyond me, Emma."

"Well, at least they're my choices," Emma mumbled under her breath.

"Excuse me, Miss Cresswell." It was Lawrence, the Cresswells' chauffeur, standing politely at the door with his hat in his hands. "We'll have to hurry to make your flight."

Emma smiled at him. "Sorry to keep you waiting. I'll be right there." She turned back to her mother. "I have to go, Mother."

"But I didn't get to tell you my surprise yet!" Kat said, pouting.

Emma sighed. "Tell me."

"No need to sound so overjoyed," Kat said reproachfully.

"The plane won't wait because you wanted to chat," Emma reminded her mother.

"All I wanted to say, darling, is that I may come up to your little island very soon. It just so happens that Buffy and Randall Arpell have a summer house there. I thought I'd pop up for a visit."

Emma mouth hung open in disbelief. She had deliberately picked a spot where no one knew her or her family. Of all the rotten luck in the world!

"When . . . when are you planning to visit?" Emma stammered.

"How about if I surprise you?" Kat asked her daughter. "Wouldn't that be fun? And we can go and do something wonderful together!"

Emma couldn't stand the hopeful look on her mother's face. Her mother always did this. She planned things with Emma and acted as if she really wanted to be with her. But then when the event actually happened, the results were always disastrous. There just really wasn't room in Kat's thoughts for anyone but herself.

"You probably won't like it there," Emma said quickly. "I mean, I don't think there's much to do," she added lamely.

Kat laughed gaily. "Oh, you know me. I can always scare up a party. And if you don't want your mother around, why, we'll just tell everyone we're sisters!"

Emma's grabbed the strap of her shoulder bag so hard that her knuckles turned white. She didn't have time to try to think of a way to prevent her mother from coming to Sunset Island. She had to catch her plane. Emma only hoped that once she arrived on the island some brilliant plan would occur to her.

"I really have to go," she said, kissing her mother's cheek carefully.

Emma was scarcely aware of the trip to the airport, nor the flight to Portland. She was too anxious about her mother's latest bombshell. If Kat showed up on Sunset Island, everything that Emma had so carefully planned would be completely ruined.

THREE

It wasn't until she got on the ferry that would take her from Portland to Sunset Island that the excitement came back. Emma stood on the topmost deck, the wind whipping her hair, and stared avidly into the distance for her first glimpse of Sunset Island. And finally, there it was, a tiny dot in the distance that grew larger and larger. The June sun warmed Emma's face and shoulders, and glinted in electric prisms off the startlingly pale blue bay.

When the ferry pulled in to dock, Emma grabbed her things and headed out. As she looked around at happy people greeting each other, overwhelming feelings of anxiety and insecurity washed over her. *Please, don't let me screw this up,* Emma said to herself. *What do I know about taking care of children? Nothing! I've never taken care of a child in my life! And what if my mother shows up? What if . . .*

Before Emma could panic herself any further, she saw the welcoming face of Jane Hewitt coming toward her.

"Hi, Emma! Welcome to Sunset Island!" Jane said, giving Emma a spontaneous little hug.

"Here, let me help you carry that," she offered, taking the bag from Emma. "The car's this way."

Emma smiled shyly at Jane, and Jane smiled back. "The kids wanted to come to meet you, but I told them no. You deserve a few minutes to catch your breath before you get bulldozed!

"I'll give you the five-cent tour on our way home, and then later on if you like we can really show you around," Jane said, as she drove. Emma stared out the window at the sights. "The island's not that big, only about forty square miles. This is the center of town," Jane pointed out, as they drove down a quaint street with white clapboard shops.

"It's so pretty!" Emma exclaimed. "It looks like an old New England town!"

Jane laughed. "Well, since that's exactly what it is, I'd say it succeeded." They stopped at a red light. "Oh, there's a place that will interest you," Jane said, pointing to a whitewashed sign with crazy letters that read THE PLAY CAFE. "That's where all the young people hang out. On weekends there's live music." Jane made a right-hand turn. "On the other side of the island there's a boardwalk on the beach," Jane continued, "with all you'd expect to find on a boardwalk. An arcade, saltwater taffy, bike rental, all that sort of thing." Emma nodded, soaking in all of Jane's information. "I've heard all the wild parties take place on that side of the island, but since we took a house here for peace and quiet— not that you'll find a lot of that with my kids—we picked a house on the bay side."

Jane pulled up to a large white clapboard house with yellow trim. Bursts of multicolored flowers sprouted in window boxes. A blue bike lay on its side in the driveway and a baby doll with blond mangled curls and only one arm sprawled on the front lawn.

"Here we are," Jane said.

"It's so . . . so homey looking!" Emma said, looking at the house with wonder.

A furiously barking golden dog with one white ear raced out of the garage, heading for the discarded doll. Running after him was a red-headed boy of about eleven.

"Dog, you come back here!" the boy screamed. The dog paid no attention. It reached the doll, took it into its teeth, and raced across the lawn.

Jane laughed ruefully. "'Homey' is a kind way to describe it," she said as they got out of the car.

The redhaired boy walked over to them. "Mom, Dog has Katie's doll again. She's going mental." The boy looked shyly at Emma.

"Emma, this is my son, Ethan. He's the oldest—eleven."

"Hi," Ethan said.

"That troublemaker over there is named Dog," Jane continued. "Katie named him. She's three. Dog is having a love affair with Katie's favorite doll. He keeps doll-napping it."

Dog trotted over to them with the doll in his mouth, his tail wagging furiously.

"Dog, give me the doll," Jane said, taking it easily from his mouth. "That's a good boy."

Ethan shook his head. "I don't know how you do it, Mom, you're the only one he'll listen to."

"What kind of dog is he?" Emma asked shyly as they headed for the house.

"He's a Heinz: fifty-seven varieties mixed together," Ethan said.

"We got him at the pound, so who knows," Jane explained.

As they got closer to the front door, Emma could hear a child crying and screaming. "That's Katie." Jane winced.

Jeff Hewitt stood at the front door holding his wailing daughter. Katie reached out to her mother and Jane handed her the doll. Katie cuddled the doll to her chest and beamed through the tears still glistening on her cheeks.

"Hi, Emma," Jeff said. "Quite the welcome you're getting."

Emma smiled at Jeff and Katie.

"This little lady is Katie," Jeff said.

Katie stuck the doll's only hand in her mouth and studied Emma solemnly.

"Hello Katie." Emma smiled at Katie.

"My name is Sally," Katie said gravely.

"The doll's name is Sally," Jane explained, "but lately Katie has decided it's her name, too."

"Well then, hello Sally," Emma said.

She was rewarded with a shy grin from Katie-Sally.

"Mom, can I show Emma her room?" Ethan asked.

"Sure, honey," Jane said, smiling at her son.

Ethan grabbed Emma's suitcase and headed up the stairs. "Follow me!" he called back to Emma.

Emma followed Ethan up two flights of stairs. "There's this really cool room in the attic," Ethan explained as they started up the second flight. "It used to be the guest room, but now it's yours."

Emma walked into a room completely decorated in blue and white. Through an open door she could see a small, white-tiled bathroom. Huge, fluffy blue towels hung on a freestanding towel rack. The ceiling sloped on one side, and a cozy window seat nestled in the gable overlooking the bay. Emma could picture herself curled up on its overstuffed cushions with a good book. The bed was covered with a quilt that was the same dainty blue-and-white pattern as the window cushions. Next to the bed on the nightstand was a blue bowl filled with yellow and white flowers, and a small white phone.

"This is just beautiful!" Emma breathed.

Ethan grinned. "I picked the flowers myself."

"Well, thank you very much," Emma told him.

Ethan shrugged. "They're from mom's garden. Don't tell her or I'm dead meat."

Emma smiled. "Your secret is safe with me," she promised.

"Hey, no fair!" Emma heard a loud voice coming up the stairs. "Mom said we all got to meet her together!" A flushed young boy of six or seven stood in the doorway, glaring at his older brother.

"So, you weren't around. What was I supposed to do, hide until you got back?"

"I just went to Stinky's," the little boy said, his hands on his hips.

"Stinky Stein is Wills's best friend," Ethan explained. "He lives next door."

"I'm Wills," the little boy said with a huge grin. He was missing his two front teeth.

Emma grinned back at him. "Pleased to meet you, Wills."

"What you are is a pain in the butt," Ethan said, correcting his little brother.

"Oh, yeah?" said Wills, blushing at his brother's insult. "Well, you're . . . you're a bigger pain in the butt."

"Oh, that's really a painful insult, Wills," Ethan said rolling his eyes. "That really hurts soooooooo bad."

There was a light tap at the doorway. "Everything okay?" Jane asked, holding Katie in her arms.

"Oh, the room is absolutely beautiful, Mrs. Hewitt. I love it," Emma told her.

"I'm glad you love it. And call me Jane."

"Put me down," Katie commanded. "I'm big."

"Gladly," Jane said, setting Katie down.

Katie walked over to Emma and stared at her. "You're pretty," she said.

Emma was charmed. "So are you," she told the little girl.

"Come on, kids, let's go downstairs and give Emma a chance to settle in. We'll eat lunch in about an hour," Jane told Emma. "After that you and I can sit down and discuss your schedule and everything, okay?"

"Fine," Emma agreed.

The Hewitts headed out of Emma's room, and Jane reached to close Emma's door behind them. "I'm really glad you're here, Emma. I think everything is going to work out great."

Emma smiled gratefully back at Jane. "Me, too."

When Jane left, Emma unpacked. She hung the few things she had brought in the closet, and put her cosmetics away in the bathroom. *Boy, I have one meager wardrobe*, Emma thought, staring at the nearly empty closet. *I'll just have to find out where kids go shopping around here.*

Shopping made her think of Sam, who claimed she was the world's greatest bargain hunter. Emma got out her address book and looked up the number Sam had given her.

Sam picked it up on the third ring.

"Jacobs residence," she said.

"Sam? It's Emma!"

"Emma! You're here!" Sam cried. "You are here, aren't you?"

"I'm here," Emma answered gaily. "I love it already!"

"I've been here for three days, and—what is it, Becky?" Sam said to someone else. "Hold on a sec, Emma, I have to do Becky's necklace. There.

33

Why do you want to wear a necklace when we're going swimming?"

"Did I catch you at a bad time?" Emma asked quickly.

"No, no, it's fine," Sam said to Emma. "Becky, go wait in the car. I'll be right there. You still there, Emma?"

"I'm here," Emma said.

"Okay, the kid is finally out of earshot," Sam said. "Whew! You wouldn't believe these twins! They're thirteen going on thirty. And they're absolutely identical. The only way I can tell them apart is Becky has a beauty mark over her lip and Allie doesn't. So when did you arrive?" Sam asked.

"Just a little while ago. This place is gorgeous!"

"Yeah, for once something in life has lived up to the advance press. Listen, I've got a ton of things to tell you, but I've got to take the monsters to their swimming lesson. Of course, Kurt, the swim teacher, is a total hunk, so it's not a complete waste of my time," Sam added.

"You're impossible," Emma said, grinning into the phone.

"I try," Sam said. "Hey, how about if we meet at the Play Café tonight after dinner? Or do you have to work?"

"I don't know, I don't have my schedule yet."

"So, look, call me later and let me know. The Play Café is—"

"I know. It's where everyone hangs out. Jane

34

pointed it out to me," Emma said. "It's only a couple of blocks from the Hewitts.

"Oh, you're on the bay side then," Sam said. "We're on the ocean side. It's very rock 'n' roll over here." Emma could hear a car honking through the phone. "It's the monsters, Emma, I have to fly. Oh, Carrie's already here, too, did I tell you that? She got here a week ago. So call me later and I'll call Carrie and we'll go out and get wild, okay?"

"Okay!" Emma agreed, hanging up the phone.

Jeff grilled burgers for lunch and the kids took turns showing off for Emma. While Ethan and Wills rinsed the dishes for the dishwasher, Jane, Jeff, and Emma went out to the back deck to talk.

"Listen, I hate to throw this at you right away," Jane said, "but we're having a big party next Friday night. Feel free to invite anyone you want, by the way, it's always a huge bash. We have it every summer."

"We always use the same caterers and they're great," Jeff added, "so there won't be much for you to do except make sure the kids get ready."

"As far as a regular schedule for the kids, the only thing that's planned is swimming lessons with Kurt at the club," Jane explained to Emma. "All the summer kids take lessons from him, and they all love him. In fact, this summer he's supposed to teach Katie to swim."

"Fat chance," Jeff said. "Katie said she won't swim until Sally learns to swim, and Sally sinks like a rock in the bathtub."

"Well, if anyone can do it, it's Kurt," Jane said with a laugh. "I think every female at the club from age three up has a crush on him—except me, of course," she added, winking at her husband.

That was the second time in three hours that Emma had heard how cute this guy Kurt was. She couldn't wait to see for herself.

FOUR

After dinner Emma changed into her jeans and a sweater and walked over to the Play Café. The place was already packed when Emma arrived. Music blared out of an old-fashioned-looking jukebox. Kids were all over the place, eating, laughing, and playing some of the many games all over the café. There was everything from video games to darts.

For a moment Emma got that awful feeling again, that she just didn't fit in and everyone could see it from a mile away. She smoothed her hair nervously and smiled shyly when a cute guy across the room grinned at her.

"Emma! Over here!" Carrie called. She was waving from a back booth.

"Hi!" Emma said, when she'd finally navigated back there. "It's so great to see you!" Emma sat down and looked around. "This place is great!" she said happily.

"I know, I love it," Carrie said. "They have the best burgers, too."

A harried-looking waitress in a Play Café T-shirt came over. Her nametag read "PATSI". "You guys ready to order?" Patsi asked them.

"Let's wait for Sam," Emma suggested.

The waitress shrugged. "Suit yourself, but this place is a zoo. I can't guarantee I'll ever make it back here again." She stuck the pencil behind her ear and hurried to another table.

"So Sam told me you've already been here a week," Emma said. "I want to hear all about it."

"Oh, it's the greatest," Carrie said. "And listen to this, you'll never believe who I'm working for."

"Who?"

"*Amigos!* Partners in crime!" Sam cried, as she reached their booth and gave them both a hug. Sam was wearing a stone-washed denim miniskirt with strategically placed rips, black tights, and her red cowboy boots. She looked casual, sexy, and fabulous. Emma made fashion notes in her head.

"Sorry I'm late. The monsters were fighting with each other over some fourteen-year-old guy at the country club." Sam sat in the booth and twisted her red hair into a ponytail. "So, did Carrie tell you who she's working for? It's unbelievable!"

"She was just about to," Emma said.

"Hey, Sam, how goes it?" The cute guy who had smiled at Emma leaned on the back of their booth. "Aren't you going to introduce me to your friends?"

"Emma Cresswell and Carrie Alden, this is Shane Treemont."

Shane grinned at Emma. "I haven't seen you around."

"Oh, I just got here," Emma said.

"Cool," Shane said. "Where you from?"

"Boston," Emma answered quietly.

"Oh yeah?" Shane said. "I go to school around there. Ever hear of Anderson-Phillips?"

Emma knew Anderson-Phillips. It was the sort of prep school that her mother sniffed at. "The really good families don't educate their children in the States, dear," she would say to Emma.

"I think I've heard of it," Emma said vaguely.

"So where do you go?" Shane pressed.

"Hey, Shane, we women of the world are no longer high-school students," Sam interrupted with a laugh.

"Oh, well excuse me," Shane said. "What if I like older women?"

"What if I told you the monsters have a crush on you?" Sam countered.

"Anything but that!" Shane said in mock horror. "Speaking of the twins, I didn't see them at the beach today."

"The monsters got sunburned yesterday so we skipped it. But you can be sure they'll be there tomorrow, lusting after you," Sam promised.

"Great," Shane groaned. He turned back to Emma. "Well, maybe I'll catch you on the beach sometime," he said, and sauntered off.

"He's kind of cute," Carrie said.

Sam shrugged dismissively. "His family has a house next door to the Jacobs. With his money and his looks he thinks he can get any girl on the island."

"Come on, Sam. Every guy on the island with money can't be a snob," Carrie said.

"Well, when I find one who's not I'll let you know," Sam said. "Now, hurry up and tell Emma who you're working for!"

"I've been trying to," Carrie said, laughing. "Okay, you know I got hired by that general manager for some people named Templeton, right? So the general manager—his name is Mr. Rudolph—he picks me up at the ferry last week, and takes me to this incredible mansion right on the ocean."

"It is a palace, I saw it," Sam confirmed.

"So before we go inside," Carrie continued, "Mr. Rudolph says perhaps he should tell me who Mr. Templeton is."

"Hurry up and tell her, I can't stand it!" Sam screamed, jumping around in the booth.

"Mr. Templeton is Graham Perry," Carrie finished.

"Graham Perry!" Sam screamed. "Carrie is working for Graham Perry!!"

"The rock star Graham Perry?" Emma asked.

"No, the milkman Graham Perry," Sam said. "Of course the rock star."

"His actual name is Graham Perry Templeton," Carrie explained. "I just couldn't believe it when Mr. Rudolph told me. I mean, the truth of the matter is, I don't even listen to rock music, I like jazz better—"

Sam groaned. "Carrie, you're from Mars or something."

Carrie ignored her. "But even I know who Graham Perry is."

"Carrie, that's fantastic!" Emma breathed. "I love that new song, 'Jump Start My Heart'."

"I haven't actually met him yet," Carrie said. "He's on tour. But his wife Claudia is really nice. She's only about twenty-five. And the kids, Ian and Chloe, are terrific."

"Tell me there's any justice in the world," Sam moaned to Carrie. "I'd give my right arm to work for a famous rock star, and you'd probably be more excited if he were a famous photographer for *Smithsonian* magazine or something."

"There, there, Sam," Carrie said with a laugh. "I promise I'll introduce you to him when he gets home."

"God, what'll I wear?" Sam asked them.

The girls cracked up just as Patsi stopped by their table again.

"Please, share the joke with me. This job is starting to drive me nuts," Patsi said.

"It looks tough," Carrie sympathized.

"Is this your summer job?" Emma asked her.

"Yeah, I'm trying to save enough money so I can spend a year bumming around Europe," Patsi sighed. "But I'm beginning to think the price is too high."

"Hey, waitress!" someone yelled from across the room.

"You're not even in my section!" Patsi yelled back. "See what I mean?" Patsi said to them.

"Maybe that's what I should do," Sam mused.

"I'd love to go to Europe. It definitely sounds more heavenly than Kansas State University."

"Right now the most heavenly thing I can think of is soaking in a hot bath," Patsi said. "You guys ordering? 'Cause it's now or never." She poised her pencil over her order pad.

"How about a pizza?" Sam suggested.

"I just ate dinner," Emma said.

"What does one thing have to do with the other?" Sam asked.

"You're right," said Emma, who had never eaten a pizza right after dinner in her entire life. "Order away."

"A large pizza, extra cheese, and three large Cokes," Sam ordered.

"Hey, y'all! Sammi!" called a lilting voice from across the room.

"Lorell. My worse nightmare," Sam groaned.

Lorell walked over to the booth along with a very thin girl with short blond hair. Lorell looked stunning in white linen pants and a pink silk T-shirt. *Why, she looks perfect,* Emma thought, *and that's exactly what Sam said about me.* "Perfect" now struck Emma as the worst look possible.

Lorell's friend looked as if she were trying desperately to look perfect, but failing miserably. She had on baggy walking shorts and a navy alligator shirt that hung on her slender frame. But it wasn't her clothes that made her look so unchic, it was the strained look around her eyes and the manic twitch to her mouth.

"Girls, this is Daphne Whittinger," Lorell said. "Daphne is a friend of mine from boarding school. Her parents have the cutest cottage on the north shore." Lorell laughed. "Can you still call a place with seven bedrooms and seven baths a cottage?"

"So who hired you, Lorell?" Sam asked.

"No one, can you believe it?" Lorell replied with indignation. "When I told Daddy he was fit to be tied. He knows lots of people who summer here, though, so he asked his friends the Popes if they wouldn't enjoy my company for the summer."

"Are you actually working for them?" Emma asked.

"We have an arrangement," Lorell explained. "They have one child, Alexa. She's twelve. She's got three tutors living at the house for the summer, so she's always studying. I just sort of act as a role model for her," Lorell explained.

"Some role model," Sam said under her breath.

Lorell's eyes fixed on Carrie. "You know, Daphne was just telling me the most amazing story," Lorell said. "Remember that funny little Mr. Rudolph who was interviewing for some mystery couple? Well, Daphne says that he was hiring an au pair for Graham Perry, and that you got the job!"

"That's true," Carrie said.

Lorell looked perplexed. "But he interviewed me, too. Why did he pick you?"

"I really don't know why he hired me," Carrie answered honestly. "But I'm glad he did."

"Ah well, *il me parait bien bizarre qu'il a prefere toi a moi.*"

Carrie just smiled blankly, but Emma automatically translated the phrase in her head: "It strikes me as rather odd that he would choose you over me."

Lorell quickly picked up on the comprehension written on Emma's face.

"Oh, I see you speak French," Lorell said to Emma. "Didn't you say you had studied in France?"

Why, she's trying to trip me up, Emma thought frantically. I never told her I studied in France! "Oh, who wants to talk about high school?" was all she said.

"Lorell, we have to go," said Daphne. Daphne pushed her hair back off her face, and Emma noticed that her hand was shaking.

"We're going to the fashion show at the club," Lorell explained. "Have a great evening!"

"I cannot stand that girl," Sam said after the two girls left.

"Something is wrong with her friend, Daphne," Emma said. "Did you see how her hands were shaking? I feel sorry for her."

"Who cares? She's a total snob!" Sam exclaimed.

"I suppose a lot of the rich kids whose parents have summer houses here are snobs," Carrie acknowledged, "but not all of them."

"Oh, no?" Sam challenged. "Then why don't they ever hang out with kids like us who work here? The fact is, we're not even allowed into the country club unless we're with someone in the family we work for."

"That's terrible!" Emma said. "Is that true?"

"Yes, it's true," Carrie said, "but I don't see why that upsets you. It's a private club and we're not members."

Emma thought guiltily about the private country club her family belonged to. It cost over a hundred thousand dollars to join.

"Now, if they didn't let people into the club because of their race or religion or something, that would be something to scream about," Carrie said reasonably.

"Yeah," Sam said sarcastically, "I guess it's okay if they only discriminate on the basis of poverty."

Carrie laughed. "Why do I think you'd look at this differently if you were rich?"

Sam laughed, too. "Why do you have to be so logical all the time?"

Emma was glad when Patsi brought their drinks. God, she could never tell her friends—especially Sam—the truth. What would they think if they knew that she'd gotten a Porsche for her sweet sixteen, or that she was probably richer than all the kids on Sunset Island they had such disdain for? *They'd probably hate me and never speak to me again, that's what*, thought Emma.

"Here's to a fantastic summer for us working stiffs!" Sam said, holding up her Coke for a toast.

Carrie and Emma raised their glasses, too.

"To the summer!" Carrie cried.

"To the summer!" Emma echoed. *And to keeping my secret*, she added silently.

The girls hung out for another hour or so, playing darts with three guys who worked as waiters at the Sunset Inn. After a while Emma forgot to worry, and then she had a fantastic time.

By the time Emma got back to the Hewitts' it was past midnight, but she felt too keyed up to sleep. She turned on the light by her bed and pulled the new journal out of her nightstand. Then she got out her calligraphy pen and began to write.

Today was my first day on Sunset Island. I love it here, but I feel so confused. Sometimes I look at myself in the mirror and I hate what I see. Here I am, eighteen years old, and this is the most daring thing I've ever done. in my life. I don't have any idea who I really am—whatever that means. I study Sam and Carrie so I can try to be more like them, but I feel like a big fake.

Emma sighed and closed her journal. *Just great*, she thought. *The first entry in my journal is a pity party for one.*

FIVE

"I don't like this bathing suit," Katie said, looking down at herself. "I like the red one."

"But this one is so pretty!" Emma exclaimed.

Katie shook her head back and forth.

Emma sighed as she helped Katie out of the yellow bathing suit. "I'll say this much for you, Katie, you are a girl with a mind of her own."

"Hey, Emma, Ethan and me want to go swimming while Katie's having her lesson, okay?" Wills stood at the door wearing a snorkel and swim fins. They were brand-new and he was anxious to try them out.

"Yeah, sure," Emma said, as she finished pulling up Katie's red bathing suit.

Katie grabbed her doll. "Sally doesn't want to swim," Katie explained with a frown.

Emma ran her fingers through her hair and tried to figure out what to do. Katie was supposed to have had her first swimming lesson two days ago, but she had absolutely refused to go.

"Why don't we take Sally with us and see if she likes it?" Emma asked Katie.

"She doesn't," Katie said. "She told me."

Ethan showed up at the door. "Come on, you

guys! I've been ready for about an hour." Then he looked over at Wills. "Wills, don't wear your snorkel and fins in the car. You'll look like a total dork."

"I like them," Wills said, wiggling his fins.

Ethan shook his head. "Please don't tell anyone you're my brother," he said, and headed downstairs.

"I don't think I like this suit, either," Katie said in a little voice.

Emma put her arm around Katie. "Sometimes it's scary to try new things," Emma said. "I'll tell you what. How about if you and Sally come with us to the pool. Then if you don't want to go in the water once we get there, you don't have to. Okay?"

"Do you promise?" Katie asked.

"I promise," Emma said.

So far, so good, thought Emma, as she drove to the country club.

Ethan and Wills ran to the main pool. Katie held Emma's hand tightly as they headed for the junior pool. When they arrived about a dozen three- and four-year-olds were milling around the pool.

Emma sat down in a chair by the pool, Katie clutching Emma with one hand and Sally with the other. "Do you want to go over there with the other kids?"

Katie shook her head no and burrowed against Emma.

Now what do I do? thought Emma.

"Hi, there," said a friendly male voice. Emma looked up into the incredibly handsome face of Kurt Ackerman, the swim teacher. "I'm Kurt," he said easily, reaching out to shake hands with Emma. Kurt was about six feet tall, with light brown hair streaked gold from the summer sun and a tanned, muscular swimmer's body.

"You must be Katie." Kurt knelt down so that he was on Katie's level.

Katie looked at him shyly. "How did you know my name?" she asked him.

"Well, I had your name on my list for Tuesday's class, but you weren't here. That's a very pretty bathing suit you have on," Kurt added.

Katie was uncharacteristically silent.

"Can I tell you a secret, Katie?" Kurt continued in his friendly voice. "I didn't learn how to swim until I was eight years old."

"That's old," Katie said gravely. "Older than my brother Wills."

Kurt nodded. "I was scared of the water. No matter what anyone said to me, I just was not going into the pool. Everyone kept pushing me, but the more they pushed me the less I wanted to try it."

Katie nodded and listened attentively.

"So finally I think everyone got sick of pushing me, and they left me alone. Then one day, all on my own, I just made a decision to try it. But I didn't try it until I decided I was ready. And then I liked it, and I wasn't scared anymore."

Emma looked at the serious expression on

49

Kurt's face. He wasn't talking down to Katie at all.

"Now it seems to me that maybe you're not ready to try the water," Kurt continued, "and that's just fine. You can watch or do whatever you want to do. And when you're ready, you just let me know. Do we have a deal?" Kurt asked, holding his hand out to Katie.

Emma could see the tension leave Katie's face as she nodded yes and shook hands with Kurt. Emma smiled gratefully at Kurt and he smiled back. *What a great guy*, Emma thought.

Katie sat on Emma's lap and watched the group of kids gather around Kurt. He talked to them for a little while, then they all put on life preservers and got into the shallow pool. Katie watched avidly as the kids learned to splash their arms and get more comfortable in the water, but she never made a move to join in. At the end of the lesson Katie was still just sitting with Emma, but at least she didn't seem so nervous anymore. Ethan showed up asking for money to buy a Coke.

Emma got money out and handed it to Ethan. "Can you take Katie with you for a few minutes, Ethan? I want to thank Kurt for helping with her."

"Sure," Ethan said. He found it much less embarrassing to be seen with his baby sister than to be seen with his little brother.

Kurt was saying good-bye to the last of the little kids as Emma waited to talk to him. She was incredibly nervous. *Just act professional,* she instructed herself. *Just ignore the fact that he's just as gorgeous as Sam and Jane said he was. You're talking to him in a strictly professional capacity.*

"I want to thank you for being so nice to Katie," Emma said. *Oh, great, I sound like Princess Di,* Emma thought with disgust.

Kurt smiled at her. *What incredibly blue eyes he has,* Emma thought. *No. Ignore his eyes, Emma.* This is a business conversation.

"No problem," Kurt said easily. "That story I told her happens to be true."

"Is it really?" Emma laughed, feeling more confident. "You mean there's hope?"

"She'll come around. You'll see. A few weeks from now we probably won't be able to get her out of the water."

Emma smiled at him and tried to think of something scintillating to say. Her mind was a complete blank.

"Well, thanks again," she finally said, turning away. *Great. I can speak five languages and I can't flirt in any of them,* Emma thought.

"Wait a minute," Kurt said, stopping her. "I told you my name but you didn't tell me yours."

"Oh, sorry," Emma said shyly. "It's Emma. Emma Cresswell."

"Emma Cresswell," Kurt repeated in a low tone. Emma thought her name had never sounded so wonderful before.

"Yes." Emma blushed. "I'm the Hewitts' au pair."

Kurt nodded. "I've been teaching Ethan and Wills for years. The Hewitts are one of the nicest summer families on the island."

"Do you live here all year?" Emma asked.

"Sure do," Kurt said. "I've lived here all my life. I love this island," he said simply.

"It's beautiful," Emma agreed.

"Most of the summer people miss the most beautiful parts of it," Kurt said. "They hang out at the club, and go from the cabana to the beach to the pool. But this is really an awesome place. Maybe I could show you the real island sometime."

Emma's heart beat a tattoo in her chest. *Act casual,* she told herself. "I'd like that," Emma said with a small smile.

"Hey, Emma, Ethan's got money. Can I have money, too?" A soaking-wet Wills stood next to Emma, still wearing his snorkel and swim fins.

Emma and Kurt burst out laughing. "Now here's a guy who took to the water," Kurt said. "Right, Wills?"

"Right!" Wills grinned. "This year I want to learn a backward somersault dive, okay Kurt?"

"You got it," Kurt promised. Wills plodded off in his fins to spend his money.

A girl of about thirteen wearing the smallest bikini Emma had ever seen pushed past Emma and pranced up to Kurt.

"Hi, Kurt! Do you like my new bathing suit?" she asked him, spinning around.

"Let's see, are you Becky or Allie?" Kurt asked playfully.

"Oh, you know," the girl said, giggling. "I'm the one with the beauty mark."

"Right!" Kurt said, snapping his fingers. "You're Allie!"

"I am not!" she said, hitting him on the arm. "I'm Becky!"

"I'm Allie!" said a voice behind Emma. Emma looked over her shoulder and saw another thirteen-year-old girl who looked just like the first one, down to an identical bathing suit. With her was Sam, wearing a bikini not much more modest than the twins.

"Emma! Fancy running into you," Sam said. "I guess you've met the monsters."

"We want to schedule a private lesson with you," Allie told Kurt, ignoring Emma.

"Sign up at the swim desk," Kurt told her. Becky and Allie scampered off, giggling hysterically.

"They aren't exactly well-mannered," Sam said, shaking her head. "I'm working on it."

"Don't they mind that you call them 'the monsters'?" Emma asked Sam.

"Are you kidding?" Sam laughed. "They consider it a compliment. They have two goals in life. Goal One: to be Bad, with a capital 'B'; Goal Two: to be kissed by their gorgeous swimming coach."

Kurt laughed. "Sorry, thirteen is a little young for me."

"Hey, Emma, there's a pool tournament at the Play Café tonight. Want to go?" Sam asked.

"I've never played," Emma confessed.

"Oh, that's okay. We can watch. Carrie says she's a ringer. I figure we can bet on her and make a fortune!"

"Okay, it sounds like fun," Emma said. She gathered up all her courage and turned to Kurt. "Would you like to come with us?"

"Yeah, I would, but I can't," he said. "I've got a part-time job driving a taxi a few nights a week, and I'm on tonight."

"Oh, well, another time, then," Emma said.

"You can count on it," Kurt replied, smiling at Emma.

Sam and Emma strolled toward the main pool. "Well, well," Sam said. "I think the hunky swimming instructor has fallen for you."

"He has?" Emma asked, her heart pounding.

"Are you kidding?" Sam snorted. "I was standing next to you in a bikini the size of three postage stamps and he never took his eyes off you."

"He's . . . he's really nice," Emma admitted.

"Forget nice," Sam snorted. "He's got buns to die for."

Emma laughed. "You're worse than the twins."

"Speaking of the twins," Sam said, looking around for them, "I better round them up before they invite half of Sunset Island over for a pajama party—and you know I don't mean the female half!"

Emma and Sam made plans to meet at the Play Café at eight o'clock, then Emma went to round up the Hewitt kids. Ethan and Wills argued all the way home over who could hold his breath under the water longer, but Emma barely paid any attention to them. She kept seeing Kurt's face as he grinned at her and said "You can count on it."

Jane and Jeff were having dinner with friends, so Emma let the kids vote on what to have for dinner. Pizza was the unanimous choice. Emma stuck one of the many pizzas that lined the freezer into the oven, and cut up a salad while the pizza cooked. She even played a game of Monopoly with the kids while they ate. By the time Jane and Jeff got home the game was almost over and the dishes were neatly stacked in the dishwasher. *Hey, I'm not bad at this!* Emma thought.

She ran up to the attic to change into her jeans. *I really do have to go shopping*, Emma thought as she brushed her hair in the mirror. *There are only so many times you can wear the same pair of jeans.*

By the time Emma got to the Play Café the big pool tournament was in progress. Emma made her way through the crowd surrounding the pool game and found Sam and Carrie at a nearby table.

"Hey, I thought you were going to play, Carrie," Emma said when she sat down.

Carrie shrugged. "I got here late. This is the final game. That guy, Butchie, is supposed to be the best pool player on the island."

Sam watched Butchie set up a shot. "I hear he's been the champ for three summers in a row," Sam said, "and his ego is as big as his pecs."

"Does he work on the island?" Emma asked.

"I think he works on a fishing boat," Sam told her.

Emma looked over at Butchie, who was just taking a shot at the corner pocket. He was tall and huge, with bulging muscles straining his shirt. His opponent was a small, slight guy with thin brown hair and thick glasses.

"That's Howie," Sam said, pointing to the little guy. "His parents have a summer house on the bay side. He goes to University of Michigan. Butchie beat him last year, too."

"How do you know so much?" Emma asked Sam.

Sam winked at Emma. "I get around."

Carrie studied the game intently. "Butchie's not that good."

"Oh, come on," said Sam, "he's made nearly every shot."

"I know what I'm talking about," Carrie insisted in a whisper. "He's not as good as he thinks he is."

Butchie called his final shot and placed the eight ball neatly in the pocket. His friends started yelling and congratulating him. "Way to go, Butchie! You're the baddest!"

Butchie walked over to Howie and held out his hand. Howie dug into his pocket and handed over a ten-dollar bill.

"Well, you beat me again this year, Butchie," Howie said good-naturedly.

"What's this ten dollars crap?" Butchie growled. "We were playing for fifty."

"No we weren't," Howie said. "We said ten."

Butchie turned to his friend, another big guy with a blond crew cut. "Hey, Larry, how much were we playing for?"

"Fifty, Butchie," Larry said with a nasty grin.

"Fifty, Howie," Butchie said, holding out his hand. "Pay up."

Butchie's oversized friends surrounded Howie. He reached into his pocket, pulled out some more money, and handed it over to Butchie. As soon as Butchie got his money, he clapped Howie hard on the back. "That didn't hurt too bad, did it, Howie? You can afford it."

Howie pushed his glasses up his nose and looked uncomfortable. Butchie shoved the money into his pants pocket and sauntered over to Emma's table.

"Hey, girls, how's it going?" Butchie asked.

"The bet was ten dollars," Sam said. "I heard you make it."

"Woah, Big Red's feisty!" Butchie yelled in a booming voice. "I like feisty women." He turned a chair backwards and straddled it, staring insolently at Sam.

57

"And besides, you're not that good," Sam added.

Emma kicked Sam under the table.

"Hey, I'm real good," Butchie shot back, reaching for Sam's thigh. She swatted his hand away.

"Would you play me?" Carrie asked Butchie.

"Like a fiddle, babe," Butchie said, laughing at his own joke.

"Pool," Carrie clarified. "I play a little."

"Nah," Butchie said. "But if you ladies want to come out drinking with us, we could have some laughs, if you know what I mean."

"How about we have some laughs at the pool table, Butchie?" Carrie asked him good-naturedly.

"Hey, give her a game, Butchie!" Larry called to him. "Show the lady how it's done."

"The thing is," Carrie said pleasantly, "I can beat you."

Butchie laughed in her face. "No way, babe."

Carrie stood up. "Humor me, then. Your bet with Howie was fifty dollars, right?" she asked Butchie.

"So?"

"Double or nothing," Carrie said. "If I win, you pay me a hundred dollars. And if you win, the three of us will go drinking with you and your buddies."

"Carrie!" Emma hissed.

The last thing in the world she wanted to do was go drinking with these Neanderthals. But Carrie stood up, all five feet four of her, and stared at Butchie.

Butchie's buddies started catcalling from across the room. "I say she beats your butt, Butchman!" one called out.

Butchie stood up and stared down at Carrie. "You're on, babe."

Butchie and Carrie went to chalk their cues, and Sam grabbed Emma's hand under the table. "I say we make a run for it," Sam advised.

"Oh sure, you were the brave one," Emma whispered, "telling him he wasn't that good." Emma looked behind her at Butchie's friends, who were leaning against the wall and grinning knowingly at her and Sam. One of them took a fifth of vodka out of his jacket pocket and poured some into his Coke, then raised it in Emma's direction and took a sip.

"Carrie better be a really, really good pool player," Emma gulped.

"You know what eight ball is?" Butchie asked Carrie.

"I've heard of it," Carrie said. "That's where one person tries to shoot in all the stripes and one person shoots in all the solids, and after that you win by calling the eight-ball shot and making it. Is that right?" Carrie asked.

"Oh God," Sam muttered, "she's not even sure how to play. We're dead."

"Right," said Butchie with a chuckle.

"Would you like to go first?" Carrie asked Butchie.

"You mean break," Butchie snorted. "It's called breaking. Ladies first, babe."

"I think you need to put up your hundred dollars first," Carrie said.

Butchie laughed and pulled out his wallet. "Sure thing, babe," he said, putting five twenties on the side of the table. "It won't be there for long." He looked over at Sam. "I got plans for you, Big Red," he said, licking his lips.

Sam smiled and said through slit teeth, "I'm going to throw up and then I'm going to kill Carrie."

Butchie racked the balls, and Carrie aimed for her first shot. A hush fell over the club as everyone gathered around to watch the game.

Thwack! Carrie sent the cue ball careening into the other balls. Two striped balls fell into side pockets.

"I guess I'm stripes," Carrie said.

"Lucky shot," Butchie grumbled.

Carrie looked over the placement of the striped balls, and then made an easy shot in the corner. Then she made another. And another. And then the shots weren't so easy, but she kept making them anyway. Butchie's friends got quieter and quieter, and Sam was grabbing Emma so hard she thought her circulation was cut off.

Amazingly, Carrie cleared the table. All that was left to sink was the black eight ball. Carrie considered her position, and then called, "Eight ball, bank shot, side pocket," and indicated which side by pointing her pool cue. Carrie leaned over and lined up her shot. *Thwack!* The cue ball banked off the side of the table and knocked into the eight ball, then the eight ball rolled perfectly into the side pocket.

There were applause and whistles as Sam and Emma went running over to Carrie. "You did it! You did it!" Sam and Emma screamed, throwing their arms around Carrie. Sam turned to Butchie. "I told you you weren't that good," she smirked.

Butchie's face turned the same red as the vinyl upholstery on the booths. "Hey, I never even got a shot," he growled.

Carrie picked the hundred dollars up from the table. "I guess I got lucky," she said mildly. She put out her hand to Butchie. "No hard feelings?"

Butchie looked like he wanted to kill Carrie, but he just turned his back and walked over to his friends. "We're out of here," he ordered. "Now."

Emma was incredulous. "Where did you learn to play like that?"

Carrie laughed. "We've got a pool table in our rec room. My brothers are fanatics. They taught me to play when I was a kid. I've even been in a few local tournaments in New Jersey."

"My God, Carrie, you could be a pool hustler!" Sam cried. "We could take you on tour and make a mint!"

"Hey, that's only the third time in my life that I ran the table," Carrie said. "I'm good, but I'm not that good."

"Excuse me, I'm Howie Lawrence. I just wanted to tell you how much I enjoyed watching that." Howie stood next to Carrie, smiling at her.

"I enjoyed it, too," Carrie said. She took two twenties from the money she had just won and held them out to Howie. "This is for you," she said.

Howie looked confused. "What? Why?"

"I only challenged him because he ripped you off and it made me mad," Carrie explained. "We heard him bet you ten dollars. So I figure you lost ten dollars fair and square, and he owes you forty dollars back. Here's the forty."

Howie took the money, a look of real admiration on his face. "Thanks. I really appreciate it," he said, pocketing the money. "What's your name?"

"Carrie Alden. And this is Emma Cresswell and—"

"Sam I know," Howie said, laughing. "I saw her on the beach and told her she looked like a model."

"And I told you to buzz off," Sam said, grinning.

"Yeah, but it was a friendly 'buzz off.' Uh, Carrie, I, uh, I hope I see you again real soon," Howie said awkwardly. "Well, be seeing ya."

"Carrie Alden, that was an extremely nice thing you did and I, for one, am impressed," Emma said.

Sam sucked down the last of her chocolate soda and blotted her red lipstick with a napkin. "I think it was stupid."

"Sam!" Emma cried.

"Not that you beat that idiot, that part was

great," Sam said. "But why did you give Howie the money?"

Carrie looked confused. "Because that ape ripped him off."

"Yeah, but Howie's family is filthy rich. He owns his own Corvette convertible. He'll never miss that money. Whereas Butchie is poor. He works on a fishing boat," Sam said.

Carrie made circles in the wet spots on the table with her fingernail. "So you mean you think it's okay to rip someone off just because they're rich?" Carrie asked incredulously.

"You're not the one who ripped Howie off," Sam reminded Carrie.

Emma could hardly believe the strong feelings welling up inside of her. *Sam was so wrong! But what right do I have to judge?* she asked herself. And it was probably true that the money meant nothing to Howie at all. Life could be so complicated!

"Anyway," Sam added, pouting, "just think of all the really cool things we could have spent that extra forty dollars on."

Carrie laughed, relieved to see that Sam was only semiserious. "Oh, now it's 'we', is it?"

"Let's at least go spend the sixty you've got left tomorrow," Sam said hopefully.

"Nope," said Carrie. "I don't know about you but I need money for school. I'm saving it."

"Bo-ring!" Sam sang.

"Anyway, there's this thing I want to go to at the Sunset Art Gallery tomorrow," Carrie said, fishing a pamphlet out of her purse. "Here it is. Tomorrow the artists are hanging the paintings and photographs for a new show that's opening next weekend. It's called 'Real and Imagined— Images of Four Artists.' The public is invited to watch them hang their work. I really want to meet Kishouru Mobishi. I think his photographs are brilliant. You guys want to come?"

Although Emma had been to all the great art museums in the world (not that she'd ever tell her friends that), she'd never seen an artist hanging his work. "Sounds interesting," Emma said. "I'll see if I can get a couple of hours off."

"I have a better idea," Sam said. "How about we go shopping tomorrow, and then we go to the actual show on Saturday and you meet him then?"

"Oh, everyone on the island will be swarming around him then," Carrie said. "This way I'll actually have a shot at talking with him about his work."

Sam sighed dramatically. "Is he cute, at least?"

Emma laughed. "Sam, you have a one-track mind!"

"As a matter of fact, he's *really* cute," said Carrie. "Look for yourself."

Sam leaned over to look at the photos of the artists in Carrie's pamphlet. "Average," Sam decreed, wriggling her nose. "Now this other guy, he's a hunk," Sam said, pulling the pamphlet out of Carrie's hands for a better look. "Oooh, this guy is hot!" Sam squealed. "'Artist Austin Payne's work in oils combines the essence of the

abstract with a sense of pared-down reality,'"
Sam read from the pamphlet. "Whatever that
means," she added. "I think I should go tomorrow
so he can explain it to me in intimate detail," she
said with a giggle.

Carrie started teasing Sam about how boy-
crazy she was, but Emma wasn't listening. It
couldn't be true! Not Austin Payne! Not her
mother's twenty-five-year-old fiancé coming to
Sunset Island tomorrow! Emma looked at the
upside down pamphlet that lay on the table. It
was Austin, all right. Same smoldering eyes,
same slicked-back hair tied into a ponytail, same
broad shoulders.

Austin Payne might or might not be talented,
but Emma was convinced he was a con artist. Kat
was always telling Emma that she should only
date guys from her own class, because then she
would know that the guy wasn't a fortune hunter.
Well, that's just what Emma thought Austin
Payne was, a con artist who wanted to marry her
mother purely for her money. Emma had a
feeling Austin Payne wouldn't want to see her
any more than she wanted to see him.

"Emma?"

"Pardon me?" Emma asked Carrie.

"I said maybe we could meet for lunch at the
Bay View, that outdoor café on the bay, and then
go over to the gallery," said Carrie.

"Oh. No. I, uh . . . I just remembered I have
to take Katie shopping tomorrow," Emma invented.

"Take her later in the afternoon," Sam suggested.

"No, no, I can't. She needs a lot of stuff."

"Are you sure you can't ask Mrs. Hewitt?" Carrie asked Emma. "It won't be as much fun without you."

Emma smiled and laughed and said all the right things, but her heart was beating frantically in her chest. Austin Payne was coming to Sunset Island. And Austin Payne could ruin everything.

SIX

"Shoot, Emma!" Katie cried, as Emma dribbled the ball toward the basket.

This was the third game of two-on-two Emma had played with the Hewitt kids, in the hope that it would take her mind off her friends' trip to the art gallery. It wasn't working, and she and Katie were about to lose their third game in a row.

Emma bounced the ball twice and then propelled it towards the hoop attached to the garage. She missed by a mile.

"You're not very good at this game," Katie decided.

"I guess you're right," Emma told Katie, giving her a hug. *And worrying about my friends meeting Austin Payne isn't helping any,* she added to herself.

"We won again," Wills declared. "That means you buy us triple scoops."

Emma nodded. They had agreed to play for ice cream at their favorite ice cream parlor, one scoop per winning game. "A deal's a deal," she agreed. "You guys wait here while I get the car keys."

Just as Emma headed into the house, the phone rang.

"Hewitt residence."

"Hi, may I please speak to Emma?" a deep male voice said.

The blood rushed to Emma's face. It sounded like Kurt Ackerman. Could he really be calling her?

"Speaking," she answered. *Oh, please don't let me sound like a librarian or something*, she prayed.

"This is Kurt Ackerman. I hope you don't mind my calling. I have the Hewitts' number in my file."

Mind??? I've only been dreaming about you since the moment I met you yesterday, she wanted to scream giddily into the phone.

"No, it's fine," Emma said. "I'm glad you called."

"I don't have to work tonight, so I thought you might like to take a drive around the island, maybe go out for a late dinner," Kurt said. "Or do you have to work?"

"No, I'm free as of seven," Emma told him, "and I'd love to."

"Great!" Kurt said. "I know where the Hewitts live. So I'll pick you up at, say, seven-thirty?"

"Fine," Emma said. "See you then." She tried not to jump up and down when she hung up the phone.

Ethan was standing in the doorway to the kitchen, scowling at Emma.

"Was that a guy?" he demanded.

"Yes, it was," Emma admitted, blushing.

"Did he ask you out on a date?"

"Yes."

"Who is he, some total dweeb?" Ethan asked.

"Kurt Ackerman," Emma told him.

Ethan scuffed his sneaker against the kitchen floor. "So? He's not so great," Ethan muttered, staring at his feet.

Ethan was acting very strange, but Emma felt too euphoric to pay much attention. She had a date with Kurt Ackerman!

In a daze, she got the car keys from the basket by the phone. Halfway out the door she stopped in her tracks. "Oh my God, what'll I wear?" she said out loud.

"Wear for what?" Wills asked her as they got into the car.

"Emma has a date with Kurt Ackerman," Ethan informed his brother. "Like it's such a big deal," he scoffed.

"Sally likes pink," Katie announced.

Emma laughed and started the car. "I'll keep that in mind, Katie."

As the kids sat in the ice cream parlor eating their triple dips, Emma decided that this very afternoon she would go shopping for some new clothes. Jane probably wouldn't mind if she took off for a couple of hours.

Emma got the kids home and cleared her idea with Jane, then headed happily to the Cheap

Boutique on Main Street. Sam had told her everyone shopped at the Cheap Boutique.

Loud rock music blared out of the sound system as Emma opened the door to the clothing store. The inside of the store looked like a nightclub. The walls were painted Day-Glo colors, and posters of various rock artists were plastered around the store. The store was packed. A tall girl stood in front of a mirror posing in a black spandex micro-mini jumper over a red spandex bra top. Another girl danced to the blaring music in an acid green miniskirt and matching crop top. Emma flashed on the many trips she'd taken with her mother to Paris and London, to see the new couture season. She and Kat would simply note the things they liked and then have them made to order. *And I never even thought twice about it,* Emma realized.

"Can I help you?" A pretty girl about Emma's age stood there, smiling at Emma. She had on a pleated navy miniskirt and a white cotton shirt under a blue and rose paisley vest.

"Yes, I'm . . . I want to buy a few things," Emma said shyly.

"Like what?" the girl asked. "Maybe I can help you."

"Well, what you have on is really cute," Emma said. "Did you get it here?"

The girl laughed. "I get everything here. That's why I took the job. So how much you want to spend?"

"The price doesn't matter," Emma said. The

70

salesgirl raised her eyebrows. "I mean, I saved up for a real shopping spree," Emma added. "I want to get a few different outfits."

"You've come to the right woman," the girl said. "Next to outfitting myself, there's nothing I love more than outfitting someone else—especially when I get a commission on the sale," she added with a grin. "My name's Beth, by the way."

Beth led Emma through the store, pointing out different dresses, skirts, and combinations that she thought would look good on Emma, until the two of them had so much stuff in their arms they could barely lug it back to a dressing room.

Emma tried on outfit after outfit. Beth was a tremendous help, and Emma had a blast. She chose the kind of clothes she'd never owned before. Some were pretty and fairly safe, but a few were really outrageous. Emma wasn't even sure she'd have the nerve to wear them. *I'll work up to it*, Emma thought, as she checked out her reflection in a cropped red leather jacket and matching red leather miniskirt. When Emma finished, Beth happily rang up the pants, skirts, dresses, tops, bathing suits, and even shoes.

Emma took out her credit card and waited for Beth to add up the total.

"Why, Emma Cresswell, how nice to run into you!" Lorell and Daphne, had suddenly material-ized next to the cash register.

"Hello, Lorell," Emma said. "Hi, Daphne."

"I see you have your own credit card," Lorell said to Emma.

"Yes. My parents just got it for me," said Emma, thinking fast. "For the summer. In case of emergency, you know."

"That comes to one-thousand nine-hundred eighty-three dollars and eighty-four cents," Beth said happily.

"Some emergency," Lorell said coolly, giving Emma a knowing smile.

"My mom said I could do some shopping," Emma said defensively.

"How sweet of her," purred Lorell. "Isn't that sweet, Daphne?"

"Sweet," Daphne said, biting off a hangnail.

These girls are hateful, Emma thought to herself.

Lorell and Daphne wandered around looking at clothes while Beth wrapped up Emma's purchases. When Beth was done, she handed Emma four huge shopping bags.

"Thanks, Emma," Beth said, "I just made more in commissions in one day than I've ever made before in a week!"

Emma thanked Beth and staggered out of the store with her packages. She could see Lorell and Daphne whispering together near the rack of leather jackets.

Emma started the car and cranked up the radio. *I'm not going to think about Lorell or Daphne or even Austin Payne, for that matter,*

Emma vowed. *I'm going to think about Kurt Ackerman, and I'm going to have fun.*

Right after dinner, Emma ran up to her room to get ready for her date with Kurt. She jumped into the shower, then ran over to her now-full closet to choose something to wear. She finally decided on a simple white cotton miniskirt with pink ribbon trim, and a matching white short-sleeved sweater. After putting on some light makeup and blow-drying her hair, Emma surveyed her image in the mirror. *Maybe this is too cutesy*, Emma thought anxiously as she stared at her reflection. But before she had a chance to second-guess herself any further, Wills was yelling up to her that Kurt was downstairs.

There is no reason to feel nervous, Emma counseled herself, as she ran downstairs. *Walk*, she commanded herself. *Act casual. Act as if you go out with guys as nice and cute as Kurt every day.*

"Hi, there," Kurt said, his eyes lighting up when he saw Emma. "You look great," he added.

"Thanks," Emma said shyly.

"He's right. You do look great," said Jeff Hewitt, who was standing in the kitchen doorway holding Katie in his arms.

"Hi, Katie," Kurt said when he saw the little girl.

"I still don't want to swim," Katie said quickly.

Everyone laughed. "That's okay, Katie," Kurt said. "You don't have to. We made a deal." He turned back to Emma. "Ready to go?"

"Have fun!" Jeff called to them as they walked out the door.

"The chariot's not too fancy, but it does the job," Kurt said, as he held open the door to his very used car.

"That's fine with me," Emma assured him. "I don't even own a car." Which was true, at the moment. She'd sold her two-year-old Porsche and wasn't planning on buying another car until the fall.

"I thought we'd head over to the other side of the island and I'd show you around. It's really beautiful," Kurt said as he started the car.

"Sounds great," Emma said. She stared at his profile as he drove, then looked away quickly. This was so much more fun that her boring dates to the "right" parties with Trent Hayden-Bishop III!

Kurt kept up a running commentary on the island as they drove toward the west shore.

"The tourists didn't discover this paradise until the forties," Kurt explained. "Before that, there wasn't much more here than a tiny village. Almost every family that lived here made their living from the lobster boats."

"How long has your family lived here?" Emma asked Kurt.

"My great-grandfather settled here in 1902, which makes us one of the oldest families on the island," Kurt said proudly. He turned down a country road just as the sun began to set.

"This is unbelievable," Emma whispered. She

stared out at the dunes, the gulls circling lazily over the water. The reflected sun made patterns of light and dark. A lone fisherman cast off from a small dock. Kurt drove off the side of the road and cut the engine. The only sound was the calling of the gulls.

For a while Emma and Kurt sat in companionable silence, neither wanting to break the spell.

"I can see why your great-grandfather settled here," Emma said finally. "And I can see why you've stayed."

Kurt smiled warmly at Emma. "That happens to be one of the nicest things you could say to me." He let his hand drift across the car seat to lightly touch the back of her neck. After the sun sank beyond the horizon, Kurt started the car up. "I'll show you the old fishing village," Kurt said. "What's left of it, anyway."

They drove down narrow streets that changed from cement to brick to cobblestone. Old weathered wooden buildings lined the street.

"My uncle Max owns that store," Kurt said, pointing to a sign that read OLD GENERAL STORE. Beyond that were small stores catering to lobstermen and fishermen, and an old café called Rubie's.

"That's it. That's all there is," Kurt said. "We could fix it up, cater to the tourists, but the truth is that we don't want the tourists to come over here, so we keep it looking shoddy on purpose." Kurt pulled into the small parking lot of Rubie's restaurant. "Get ready for the best seafood you ever tasted in your life," Kurt promised. "You do like seafood, don't you?"

"I love it," Emma said happily.

As they entered the café a robust woman with flaming red hair came out from behind the cash register. She was as tall as Sam but twice as wide. She wore jeans, a flannel shirt, and a huge grin. She enveloped Kurt in a bear hug.

"Kurt, you devil, where've you been keeping yourself?" the woman said.

"Between two jobs and summer school I keep busy," Kurt answered with a grin.

"Yeah? Too busy for your old friends now that you're a college boy?" Rubie asked, hands on her impressive hips.

"Never too busy for you, Rubie. I want to introduce you to my friend. Rubie, this is Emma Cresswell. Emma, my adopted mother Rubie O'Mally."

Rubie shook hands warmly with Emma. "Nice to meet you, Emma. Any friend of Kurt's is welcome here." She looked Emma over. "You're cute as can be, but you could use some fattening up," she decided. "Sit down, you two. It's time for a Rubie feast!"

They started with two dozen steamers and then polished off two steaming bowls of the best clam chowder Emma had ever tasted. Kurt spoke easily about his family. His mom had died four years ago—at which point Rubie had unofficially "adopted" him. He lived just two blocks from Rubie's restaurant with his dad and his two sisters, Lindsay and Faith. He was a sophomore at University of Maine, Portland-Gorham campus.

"Everyone calls it Po-Go," Kurt told Emma.

"What are you studying?" Emma asked as Rubie proudly set two steaming cod filets on their table.

"Sciences mostly," Kurt said. "What I want to do is to go into sports medicine. How's the cod?"

Emma savored her first bite. "This is heavenly!" she said. "So what kind of a degree do you need to go into sports medicine?" Emma asked.

"Hey, I'm pretty good at talking about myself, but I'd appreciate it if you'd share the wealth," Kurt said with a grin.

Emma blushed. She really was interested in getting to know Kurt, but she also desperately did not want to talk about her life. Talking meant evading the truth or outright lying, and Emma didn't want to do either.

"Well, there's not much to tell," Emma said quietly. "I'm from Boston. I just graduated from high school. It's not very interesting," she added lamely.

"Everything about you interests me," Kurt said softly. "There's just something about you. . . ." Kurt studied Emma thoughtfully. "You look very cool and together, but you seem . . . shy at the same time."

Emma blotted her lipstick on her napkin and took a sip of water. This conversation was skating on thin ice. "What is this, analyze Emma night?" she asked lightly.

"Hey, I'm sorry," Kurt said, reaching across the table to touch her hand. "I hate it when people do that to me. Forget I said anything."

"So, how much do you love the cod?" Rubie asked them, standing over the table.

"It's the best," Emma said.

"Smart girl," Rubie said with a wink. "You can bring her around more often!"

After they had coffee and shared a piece of Rubie's homemade cheesecake, Kurt suggested a walk on the beach.

"Sounds great," Emma agreed.

Rubie refused to let Kurt pay for the dinners, and kissed them both good-bye at the door. "Don't be a stranger!" she said, wagging her finger at Kurt.

"How could I stay away from you, Rubie?" Kurt said, giving her a hug.

Kurt took Emma's hand and led her down steep steps to the beach. They took off their shoes to walk in the sand.

"There's a million stars up there," Emma said softly, staring at the sky.

"Yeah. Somehow the stars and the ocean put things in perspective for me," Kurt said. "When I'm feeling overwhelmed, I just come out here at night, and then everything looks different."

"What do you feel overwhelmed about?" Emma asked him.

Kurt shrugged. "Oh, you know, the usual stuff.

Can I save up enough money to stay in school, can I work and still have enough time to study, can I get to know the mysterious Emma Cresswell. . . ."

"I'm not mysterious!" Emma laughed.

"Okay, then, tell me where you'd like to be five years from now," Kurt challenged.

"Five years? That's forever!" Emma protested. "Okay. I'd like to be in Africa," she blurted out.

Kurt stopped walking and looked at Emma. "Africa?"

"Does that seem crazy? Maybe it is crazy—"

"No, no, it's not crazy. I'm just surprised, that's all," Kurt said.

"I . . . I'd like to study wildlife, you know, endangered species. And I think I'd like to join the Peace Corps," Emma confessed.

"Well, well," Kurt murmured with admiration, "you really are full of surprises."

Emma could feel Kurt's eyes on her, and she was filled with guilt. Sure, she had blurted out the truth. She really did dream of joining the Peace Corps and going to Africa. Of course, her parents would sooner commit her to a home for the mentally deranged, so Emma hadn't exactly mentioned it to them. Their idea of foreign travel involved the family's private jet and four-star hotels. And to be honest, that was the only kind of travel Emma knew, too.

"It's just an idea," Emma said, as they started walking again. "I'll probably never do it."

"Hey, I believe we create our own destiny,"

Kurt said seriously. "If you want it, you should go for it."

Emma smiled into the darkness. "I'll keep that in mind." Something in the sky caught her eye. "Look! A shooting star!"

"Make a wish!" Kurt ordered.

Emma closed her eyes. *I wish he would kiss me*, she thought. When she opened her eyes Kurt was staring at her. She could just barely make out his face in the starlight.

"What did you wish for?" he asked softly.

"I thought I wasn't supposed to tell," Emma whispered.

"Ah, an honorable woman," Kurt said. "My favorite kind."

He gently stroked her hair. Then he drew her face to his, and kissed her lightly. Pulling back from her, he stared at her face a moment, then he kissed her again. Only this time his arms went gently around her, and she gave herself up completely to the incredible, fabulous feeling of kissing him back.

Well, well, Emma thought. *I guess wishes on shooting stars really can come true.*

And she kissed him again.

SEVEN

"Lobster woman!" Sam sang out, and let her beach bag rest lightly on top of Emma's head. Emma looked up at Sam and Carrie.

"She's right," Carrie agreed. "You better put on some more sunblock. You're back's turning red. I'll do it for you," Carrie offered. She plopped down on the blanket next to Emma and pulled the sunblock out of her bag.

It was the day after Carrie and Sam had gone to the art gallery, the day after Emma's date with Kurt. Emma had been so caught up in thinking about Kurt, she'd actually managed to temporarily banish all thoughts of Austin Payne from her mind. Since all three girls had a few hours off in the afternoon, they had agreed to meet at the beach. Emma had been so excited to tell her friends about Kurt, but now that they were actually together, all the horrible anxiety about Austin Payne crept over her again.

"You're skin is so pale, you really have to be careful," Carrie told Emma, putting away the sunblock.

"Not me," Sam said, finding a good position on

the blanket. "Ah, the sun feels great," she sighed. "Bliss."

"You must be the only real redhead on the planet capable of tanning," Carrie told Sam. "You're already copper colored."

Sam shrugged. "Maybe I have Indian blood. Hey, Em, you missed a great time yesterday," she added.

"Oh, really?" Emma asked, trying to sound nonchalant.

"Yeah, we had a blast," Sam said, as she put on her sunglasses and settled her hands under her head. "Artists are great. They're so . . . artsy."

"I couldn't believe I was standing there, watching Kishouru Mobishi hang his photographs," Carrie said in an awed voice. "I mean, we studied his work in my photography class last year, and I actually got to talk to him!"

"Sort of," Sam qualified. "He doesn't speak a lot of English."

Carrie laughed. "He does, too. He just has an accent. Anyway, I noticed you understood him when he said that he'd like to photograph you some time."

"He was just flirting with me," Sam said in a worldly tone of voice. "If he'd been serious I'd have this bod draped in front of his camera right this minute."

"Everyone was flirting with Sam," Carrie said, turning over onto her back.

"Hey, you had your share of attention," Sam reminded Carrie. "It's that Ivory girl look you have. You're going to look like a virgin until you're a grandmother—guys love that."

Carrie laughed. "I don't think it's medically possible to become a grandmother and still be a virgin."

"Ha ha," Sam said, and pulled down the straps of her bikini top to avoid tan lines. "Anyway, Emma, we really did have a blast. These guys were seriously cute. Especially that guy Austin Payne. He was even cuter in person than he looked in his picture."

Emma was glad her sunglasses were hiding her eyes. *I don't want to hear about this*, she was screaming inside! *I don't want to hear about Austin Payne and I don't want to be anywhere near Austin Payne!*

"And what a flirt!" Sam continued. "He's got those real soulful kind of eyes, you know? He put one hand on the wall over my head, stared at me with those sexy eyes, and told me he was studying my face."

"He told her she had a 'bedroom body,'" Carrie reported.

My mother's fiancé was flirting with my friend, Emma thought wildly. *That is disgusting! Okay, don't jump to conclusions*, she counseled herself. *It means he's a cretin, but it doesn't necessarily mean he's a cheat.*

"So what did you say back?" Emma asked Sam. "I mean, don't you think that's a stupid line?"

"Believe me, he's so cute he can get away with it," Sam said. "All I could think about was what great hands he must have, being an artist and all."

"Actually, I had quite an interesting experience yesterday myself," Emma said, happy to change the subject. "Last night, more specifically," Emma said.

"Like what?" Sam asked.

"Like I went out with Kurt Ackerman."

Sam sat up and took off her sunglasses to look at Emma. "You did not." She looked at Emma's smiling face. "You did!" She turned to Carrie. "She did!"

"Tell us all about it!" Carrie demanded. "When did he ask you out?"

"Did he call you and actually ask you on a date, or did you just, like, run into him?" Sam wanted to know.

"He called me and asked me out to dinner," Emma said. "He said he wanted to show me a part of the island that tourists don't usually see."

"Like what," Sam asked, "his bedroom?"

Carrie hit Sam playfully. "Shut up and let her tell it!"

Emma sat up to talk. "It was so fabulous," she said, remembering and hugging her knees to her chin. "We drove around, then we parked to watch the sun set over the dunes."

"Wow, he works fast," Sam remarked.

"No, it wasn't like that," Emma said. "He was a perfect gentleman."

Sam put her sunglasses back on. "What a drag."

Carrie put her hand over Sam's mouth. "Go on, Emma. Sam promises to shut up. Don't you, Sam?" Carrie took her hand off of Sam's mouth and waited.

"I'll be good," Sam promised solemnly, "but get to the juicy parts."

"Well, after we watched the sunset we went to this incredible restaurant called Rubie's for seafood. Rubie is sort of Kurt's adopted mother," Emma explained. "His real mother died four years ago."

"Wow, he must really like you to take you to his adopted mother's restaurant on your first date," Carrie commented.

"It's terrible about his mom," Sam added.

Emma nodded. "I think they were really close. Anyway, after dinner we went for a walk on the beach—"

"Ah ha!" cried Sam. "The juicy part!"

"We talked and talked," Emma said dreamily. "And then he kissed me."

"Kissed you like your Uncle Herbie would kiss you or kissed you like *major kiss?*" Sam asked.

"Major kiss!" Emma said, laughing. "Actually, a lot of major kisses!"

"Wow! Oh, this is awesome," breathed Sam. "I mean, Kurt is big-time cute—and you know I have the highest of standards."

"Right," Carrie agreed. "The guy's got to be breathing, for example."

"Hey, I happen to be very discriminating," Sam

said haughtily. "Kurt is at least a B, B plus on the hunk-ola scale."

Emma shook her head at Sam. "So what's an A?"

Sam put her hands behind her head languidly. "Oh, let's see . . . Austin Payne is an A."

"Oh, please!" Emma sputtered before she could stop herself.

"What do you mean 'Oh, please'?" Sam asked. "You haven't even met him!"

Emma had to think fast. "I just meant . . . he's old, isn't he?"

"I prefer to think of him as ripe," said Sam, wiggling her eyebrows at Emma.

"Now aren't you sorry you asked?" Carrie said.

Sam looked at her watch and groaned. "I have to go. I'm taking the monsters to the movies this afternoon. They happen to know that two fifteen-year-old guys they like are going to be there." She stood up and stretched. "Hey, Howie Lawrence is giving a party tonight. He told me to invite you guys. Especially you, Carrie."

"Yes to the party, no to Howie," said Carrie.

"How about you?" Sam asked Emma. "Or do you have a date with Mr. Wonderful?"

"Last night was only my first date with him," Emma reminded Sam. "We're not a couple or anything."

"So you'll come to the party?" Sam asked.

"Sure," Emma said.

"I can pick you guys up," Sam said. "Mr. Jacobs

is going to be home tonight. I already asked if I could use the car."

"Nice guy," Carrie commented, stuffing her towel into her beach bag.

"Yeah, too nice a guy to handle the twins," Sam said ruefully.

"I can drop you two off," Emma offered, since Carrie and Sam had walked over to the beach. They all got in the car.

"What's the story with Mr. Jacobs?" Carrie asked Sam. "I mean, where's Mrs. Jacobs?"

"No one says, exactly," Sam said. "But reading between the lines, I think she ran off with some musician who's like half her age and gave custody of the girls to their father."

"That's terrible!" Carrie exclaimed.

"No kidding!" Sam agreed. "No wonder the twins are so crazy! Look what they've got for a role model!"

Emma kept her mouth shut. The twins story sounded too much like her own story. She hadn't had a very good role model, either. Austin Payne was soon going to be her stepfather. Emma shuddered at the thought.

"You cold?" Carrie asked her.

"I guess I got a chill on the beach—from the sun," Emma said.

"Well, don't get sick, because this party tonight should be great," Sam said. "I hear Howie's house is not to be believed."

Emma dropped her friends off and headed back to the Hewitts'. Ethan and Wills had just returned from their swimming lesson at the club. Emma had been disappointed when they told her that Stinky Stein's mom was driving them. She wanted an excuse to see Kurt again.

"Hi, guys," Emma said. "How was swimming?"

"Great!" said Wills, enthusiastic as always. "I'm learning to dive."

"How about you, Ethan?" Emma asked him. Ethan had been quiet and sullen all morning.

"It was okay," Ethan said.

"Is Kurt teaching you to dive, too?"

"I happen to already know how to dive," Ethan said. "Kurt doesn't have to teach me."

"Well, that's great," Emma said. She wanted to ask Ethan what was bothering him, but she knew she shouldn't ask him in front of Wills.

"I'm going upstairs to change," Emma told them. "Where's Katie?"

"She's in the backyard with Dad," Wills said.

"Okay, I'll be right down."

Emma ran up to her room and changed into a pair of jeans and a T-shirt. Just as she was brushing her hair, there was a knock on the door.

"Come on in," Emma said.

Ethan stood at the door, holding a small gift-wrapped box. He came into Emma's room and sat on her bed.

"So did you have fun last night?" Ethan finally asked Emma.

"Yes, I did. Kurt's a really nice guy, don't you think?" Emma asked Ethan.

Ethan just shrugged and stared at the floor. "What did you do?"

"We went out to dinner."

Ethan asked a few more questions, which Emma answered patiently. Finally Ethan stood up and walked quickly to the door, leaving the clumsily wrapped box on the bed. "That's for you," he said, as he practically ran out the door.

Emma opened the box to find a beautiful white silk scarf shot through with gold embroidery thread. She knew it had to be expensive. And then the light dawned. *Oh my*, thought Emma, *Ethan has a crush on me! What a dope I was not to realize it!*

Emma ran downstairs to look for Ethan. She found him sitting by himself in the den, reading a comic book.

"Ethan, I want to thank you for the beautiful scarf. You've got wonderful taste."

Ethan shrugged and concentrated fiercely on his comic book.

"It must have cost you a lot of money."

Ethan shrugged without looking up.

"You must have had to really save up your allowance to be able to afford that scarf," Emma said carefully. She knew Ethan got five dollars a week allowance. And she knew that this scarf had to cost more than ten times that.

"I gotta go to Dave's house," Ethan said, naming his friend from across the street. "See ya."

Emma sat for a minute, watching Ethan as he

darted out of the house. She had a bad feeling in the pit of her stomach, a feeling that Ethan was lying to her. Where did he get the money to buy that scarf? And what should she do about his crush on her?

That evening, Emma happily surveyed her full closet to choose an outfit for Howie's party. She fingered the red leather mini, but decided she simply didn't have the nerve to wear it. *Not yet, anyway*, Emma mused, giggling to herself. *Who knows what the future will bring?*

Emma decided on a peacock blue cotton and lycra mini shift dress with a matching belt, and flat white sandals. She pulled them out of the closet just as the phone rang.

"Hello?"

"Hi, Emma. It's Kurt."

Her heart beat more rapidly at the sound of his voice.

"Oh, hi Kurt. How nice to hear from you."

Emma winced at her own voice. *Why do I always sound like I'm on my way to a garden party?* "I mean, how's it going?" Emma added. *There*, she thought, *that's better*.

"Fine," Kurt said. "I didn't see you at the boys' swimming lesson today, so I just wanted to call and tell you I had a really great time last night."

"Oh, me, too!" Emma breathed.

"So are you bringing Katie to the pool tomorrow?" Kurt asked.

"Yes, but she tells me she's still determined not to swim."

"That's okay," said Kurt. "She'll come around if we don't push her, you'll see."

They chatted for a while longer and then hung up. Emma kept hoping that Kurt would ask her out again, but he didn't. *Maybe he'll ask me when I take Katie for her lesson tomorrow,* Emma thought to herself. *Or maybe he just called to be nice and he just wants us to be friends. Or maybe . . . No. I'm not going to make myself crazy with "or maybes." I'm going to see Kurt tomorrow, and I'm going to a party tonight and I'm going to have fun.*

Sam was only a half hour late—which for Sam meant on time—to pick up Emma. Carrie was already in the car.

"You two look great," Emma said as she got into the car. Carrie had on black baggy pants, a white T-shirt and a black and white paisley vest. Sam had on a red leotard underneath a navy blazer, skintight faded jeans, and her red cowboy boots.

"So do you," Carrie told her. "Very cute dress."

"Thanks. I bought a few things at the Cheap Boutique." Emma just prayed that Lorell wouldn't run into Sam and Carrie and tell them just how much.

The party was in full swing when the girls arrived. Loud rock music blared from a fabulous stereo system and lots of kids were dancing in the huge sunken living room. As Sam had predicted, the house was spectacular. The entire back of the house was glass, offering a spectacular view of the ocean.

As soon as the girls walked in the door, Howie made a beeline towards Carrie. Sam saw him coming from across the room.

"Here comes lover boy," Sam whispered to Carrie.

"Hi, welcome," said Howie as he grinned at Carrie. He had to practically scream over the loud music.

"Hi yourself," Carrie yelled back good-naturedly. "Great music. What record is that?"

"Flirting with Danger," Howie said. "They're a great local band." Howie looked around the room. "See that guy over there?" he said, pointing to a great-looking long-haired guy talking with a girl in the corner of the room. "That's Billy Samson. He's the lead singer. This is their demo. They're shopping it around," Howie explained.

"So where did you get it?" Sam yelled over the music.

Howie grinned. "My dad's an executive at Polyphonic Records," he said. "I can get anything." He turned to Carrie. "Want to dance?"

"Sure," Carrie said. Howie grabbed Carrie's hand and led her to the dance floor. She looked back once at her friends and shrugged good-naturedly.

"Why does he have to be so rich and such a dweeb?" Sam asked Emma.

"He doesn't seem so bad," Emma murmured.

"Let's go get a drink," Sam said. "I need a beer."

They found beers in the bathtub, sitting in tons of crushed ice. "Very efficient," Sam said, grabbing two of them and handing one to Emma.

Emma loved good wine or good champagne, but she'd never actually drunk a beer in her life. "No, thanks," Emma said. "I think I'll find a Coke. Beer gives me a headache after I've been in the sun," she improvised.

The two girls wandered back into the living room. Sam eyed Billy Sampson, deep in conversation with a very sexy blonde who kept trying to maul him instead of talk to him.

"Look at that," Sam said. "Is that girl obnoxious or what?"

The girl had her hand inside his denim shirt and was rubbing small circles with her fingers. Billy gently extricated her hand and continued talking.

Sam downed a big gulp of beer, still looking over at them. "That guy is gorgeous, though. I have to admit."

Emma looked at Billy dubiously. "He's handsome, but I just can't get used to a ponytail on a man."

"I think it's sexy," Sam said. "If someone would stick Goldilocks over there back in her cage, I'd go introduce myself."

"Having a good time?" A thin, dark-haired guy wearing sunglasses smiled at Sam and Emma. With him was a fair-haired shorter, younger guy

93

with chubby cheeks and a stubborn cowlick. The younger guy had a camera slung around his neck. Both guys were overdressed to perfection in designer jackets and silk shirts.

"Sure," said Sam. "What's not to like?"

The dark-haired guy slowly pulled his sunglasses down and looked them both over carefully, then he put the sunglasses back in place. "Do you two beauties have names?" he yelled over the music.

"I'm Sam Bridges."

"Emma Cresswell."

"I'm Flash Hathaway. This is my assistant, Leonard Fuller."

Leonard smiled ingratiatingly at the girls.

"What does he assist you with?" Emma asked curiously.

Flash tapped the camera slung around Leonard's neck.

"I'm a fashion photographer," Flash said with a cool smile.

As if on cue, Leonard eagerly reached into his breast pocket and pulled out a leather business-card folder. He extracted two cards and handed them to Sam and Emma.

Sam's face lit up when she read the card. "You're with Universal Models?" she asked in awe. "They're famous!"

Emma looked at the business card, then back at Flash and Leonard. She, too, had heard of Universal Models. In fact, she knew a girl from boarding school who had done some modeling for them in Paris and Milan. Still, she got a very creepy feeling from this guy Flash.

Flash smiled enigmatically at Sam. "Have you ever been told that you should be a model, Sam?"

"Once or twice," Sam said nonchalantly.

Flash nodded. "You've got the height, the bones, the bod. I'd say you're a natural."

"Really?" said Sam, totally thrilled.

"So Mr. Hathaway," Emma said, unable to bring herself to call *anyone* "Flash", "what are you doing on Sunset Island?"

"I scout here now and then," he said, still eyeing Sam. "Want to dance, babe?" he asked her.

"Sure!" Sam said. Flash took her hand and they joined the writhing bodies in the dance pit.

"Dance?" Leonard asked Emma hopefully.

Emma, who had been taught to be polite above all else, could not think of a good excuse to say no to Leonard.

"All right," she agreed graciously.

Leonard eagerly led Emma to the dance pit. A fast song with a great beat was playing, and Emma began to dance conservatively to the music. Leonard began to throw his body around, gyrating and spinning. His hands weaved through the air and his feet beat a tattoo into the polished wood of the dance pit. The fact that he was not on the beat didn't seem to dampen his enthusiasm.

"I'm known for my dancing!" Leonard

screamed in Emma's face as he circled around her.

Oh, no! Now Leonard was dropping to the floor in splits, then jumping back up to wave his arms around. *I've got to escape*, Emma thought. *I wish the song would end. I wish Kurt Ackerman would walk through the front door.* Just then Emma looked towards the door as it opened. And in walked Austin Payne with his arm around a gorgeous brunette in a skintight blue dress.

Emma gasped out loud. "Sorry, babe!" Leonard yelled, apparently thinking he had stepped on her foot.

"I've . . . I've got to go!" Emma said, and ran off the dance floor toward the back of the house.

"Hey!" Leonard called after her, but she didn't care what he thought. Or what anyone thought. All she cared about was making sure that Austin didn't see her.

Emma ran down a hallway and opened the first door she came to. It was a bedroom. On the bed a couple were locked in a serious embrace.

"Excuse me," Emma murmured hastily and backed out.

She tried the next door. Fortunately it was a bathroom and fortunately it was unoccupied. Emma quickly ran in and locked the door behind her. She looked at her face in the mirror. She was white as a ghost. *Great*, Emma thought ruefully. *What am I supposed to do, stay locked in a bathroom all night?*

She splashed cold water on her face while she

tried to plan a way out of the house. *I can't just leave my friends without saying anything*, Emma thought wildly. *They'll call the police or something*. Then a thought occurred to her.

She pulled Flash's business card out of her purse and rummaged around for a pencil. No such luck.

Emma looked around the bathroom for inspiration, and finally opened the medicine cabinet over the sink. There was nothing in there but a bottle of aspirin and some cosmetics. Eye shadows, blushes, lipsticks, eyeliner pencils . . . pencils! Aha! Emma thought triumphantly. She took a brown pencil from the medicine cabinet, apologizing in her head to the owner of the cosmetics she was ruining.

SAM, (Emma wrote on the back of the business card), GOT A HEADACHE & GOT RIDE HOME WITH FRIENDS. CALL YOU TOMORROW. TELL CARRIE. EMMA.

So far, so good, Emma thought, slipping the eyeliner back into the medicine cabinet. *Now who do I get to deliver the note?*

Emma took a deep breath and opened the door to the bathroom. She stuck her head out the door to make sure no one she knew was in the hallway. A short girl said, "Excuse me," and slipped into the bathroom behind Emma. The next person she saw was Howie. Unfortunately he saw her, too.

"Emma! Hi! Having a good time?" Howie asked her.

"Yes, it's a great party," Emma said, trying to put some enthusiasm in her voice.

"Hey, your friend Carrie is really nice," Howie said earnestly. "I mean, a really great girl. Do you think she'd go out with me?"

Emma forced herself to breathe deeply and to speak normally. "I don't know, Howie. You'd have to ask her."

Howie looked crestfallen. "I did. Twice. So far it's no go. Does she have a boyfriend or something?"

"Uh, maybe. Could you excuse me, Howie? I . . . have to go in here." She pointed to the door behind her.

Howie looked confused. "The linen closet?"

Emma laughed a manic laugh. "Is that the linen closet? No, of course I didn't mean the linen closet. I meant . . . that bedroom. I left something in there."

Emma opened the door to the bedroom and shut it behind her, pressing her body against the back of the door. The couple was still on the bed. More correctly they were now *in* the bed, their clothes in a pile on the floor. They seemed much too involved to notice the door opening. Emma shut her eyes quickly and ducked down to floor level.

Okay, thought Emma. *I am crouched on the floor of someone's bedroom while people I don't know are doing what I can only guess on the*

98

other side of the room. Outside the door is Howie and beyond him is Austin Payne. I definitely have a problem.

Emma counted to one hundred in her head and slowly opened the door again. No Howie. She slid out the door and was about to take a step down the hall when around the corner came Austin and the brunette.

Emma plastered her body back against a small recess in the wall where a beautiful sculpture sat on a marble pillar. From that vantage point she saw Austin take the brunette's hand and lead her into a bedroom. Emma thought she saw Austin caress the girl's hip before he closed the door. She definitely heard the girl giggle in response.

Emma darted out from her hiding place and ran down the hall. A girl with a familiar face walked by.

"Beth!" Emma cried.

"Oh, hi, Emma!" Beth said. "Hey, you're wearing one of the dresses you got at the boutique. It looks great!"

"Listen, I wonder if you could do me a favor?" Emma asked.

"Sure."

"See that tall girl with the red hair dancing down there?"

"Sam?" Beth said. "I know her. She shops at the boutique all the time."

"Could you please give her this?" Emma handed Beth Flash's business card. "I'm . . . not feeling very well, and I just can't bear the thought of negotiating the dance floor," she explained.

"Okay."

"Thanks a million," Emma said.

Emma headed to the back, or ocean side, of the house, hoping to find an exit. Through a study and down a hallway, Emma found a small laundry room with a door leading out to the ocean. Success!

Emma headed for the boardwalk, where she knew there was a trolley that took people from one side of the island to the other. Fortunately a trolley was just getting ready to pull away, and she hopped on and headed for the bay side.

When Emma got home she headed straight to her room. As she got undressed all she could think about was how close she had come to blowing everything. All her friends had to do was find out that Austin Payne was her mother's fiancé. That would be the beginning of the end. *I have a right to live my own life!* Emma thought fiercly, as she climbed into bed with her journal.

Tonight everything was almost completely ruined. I must not let Austin Payne know I'm on Sunset Island. I hate being forced to lie and to sneak around, but there's no other way. The worst part is, I think Austin is fooling around behind my mother's back. I wish he'd just drop dead. Okay, maybe not drop dead, just drop off the edge of the earth.

At least off the edge of Sunset Island. And my mother thinks she loves the creep. Once she thought she loved my father, too. Maybe there really is no such thing as love at all.

EIGHT

Emma stood in front of her mirror and stared at herself critically in her new pink bathing suit. Four suits she had already tried on lay on the floor of the bathroom. Carrie and Sam sprawled on Emma's bed eating popcorn. It was the night after Howie's party.

"So which one should I wear tonight?" Emma asked them anxiously.

That morning Kurt had invited her to the staff's midnight swim party at the club that evening. Sam and Carrie were going, too. Sam had been invited by Kip Prescott, the head lifeguard, and Carrie had been invited by Howie Lawrence. Why Howie Lawrence was going to a staff party when he didn't work at the club, no one knew.

Carrie had no desire to go out with Howie, but her friends convinced her that it would be fun with all three of them there. They were meeting the guys at the club.

"Well, that suit is cute," Sam said, "but the black fishnet bikini is killer."

"I don't think I have the nerve to wear the black bikini," Emma admitted.

"I vote for the white one, absolutely," Carrie said. "It's sexy and classic."

"Are you sure?" Emma asked anxiously. "Maybe I should try it on again." She rushed back into the bathroom to change once more.

"I don't know why you're so worried," Sam called in to Emma. "Kurt has eyes for no one but you, dahlink."

Emma came out of the bathroom and pirouetted before her friends. "What do you think?" she asked, as she adjusted the halter neck.

"That's the one," Carrie confirmed.

"Yeah, I agree," Sam said, scrutinizing Emma carefully. "The high cut makes your legs look longer, and the white against your pale skin sort of heightens that ice maiden effect."

Emma looked anxiously into the mirror, then back at her friends. "Do I look too pale?"

Sam groaned. "And I thought I was bad about changing my clothes a zillion times. Relax! It looks great on you. The black one is more drop-dead, but this one is more you."

Emma sat on the cushions beneath her window. "It's just that . . . I really like him," Emma said softly. "I want him to think I look great."

Carrie groaned and fell back on Emma's pillows. "I'm so jealous. Sam has a date with Kip, who looks like Tom Cruise, and you have a date with Kurt, who is incredibly nice and incredibly cute, and I have a date with Howie Lawrence."

"Oh, come on," Sam objected. "I'm not seriously interested in Kip. He's totally conceited."

"That's because he's great-looking and he knows it," Carrie said, "even if he doesn't seem to have a discernable I.Q.—no offense, Sam."

Sam shrugged. "I'll be brutally honest. I'm not going out with him for his I.Q.," she said, finishing the last of the popcorn. "Oh, listen, Em, speaking of great-looking, I forgot to tell you. Guess who showed up at Howie's party after you left?"

"Who?" Emma asked as she crossed to the bathroom to change. *As if I didn't know,* she said to herself.

"Austin Payne, that artist I was telling you about," Sam called in to Emma. "Just when I was going to try to find you to introduce you to him, Beth gave me your note."

Emma came out of the bathroom wearing a long T-shirt. She put her extra bathing suits into a drawer and put the white one in her beach bag. Then she opened her closet to pick out an outfit to wear over to the club.

"Wow, you really did get a lot of new stuff," Sam said. She jumped off the bed to look more closely. "This red leather outfit is fabulous!" Sam decreed. "I remember seeing it in the Cheap Boutique, it cost a mint!"

"Yeah, I guess I sort of splurged," Emma said, hastily closing the closet door. "I think I'll just wear jeans and a shirt," Emma said, pulling her jeans from a drawer.

Emma brushed her hair while Sam fixed her makeup in the mirror. Carrie painted her nails with the clear polish sitting on the vanity table.

"You know, I just realized something," Carrie said as she waved her nails around to dry. "This is my first date with anyone besides Josh in my entire life."

Sam stopped putting on her lipstick and turned to Carrie. "You mean you've only ever dated one guy?"

"That's right," Carrie said.

"Ever?" Sam asked. "I mean ever, ever?"

"Ever, ever," Carrie said, tightening the top of the nail polish. "Josh and I became a couple in eighth grade. I can't believe the first date I have with another guy is with Howie Lawrence."

"That is sort of pathetic," Sam agreed.

"Don't think of it as a date," Emma suggested. "Think of it as a bunch of friends hanging out together."

"Sometimes I dream about meeting some incredible new guy, someone really exciting," Carrie said, "and sometimes I think I must have been out of my mind to break up with Josh. He loves me, and he's a great guy."

"Yeah, but one guy since eight grade?" Sam said, making a face. "You don't even have any basis for comparison." She looked back at herself in the mirror. "Do I have too much lipstick on?"

"Just blot it," Emma suggested, handing Sam a tissue. "You two ready to go?"

"As ready as I'll ever get," Carrie said with a sigh.

When the girls arrived at the club, they changed and dropped their stuff off in the women's locker room and then headed for the pool. Howie saw Carrie from across the room and his face lit up as if it were Christmas. Kurt came up behind Emma and lifted the hair gently off the back of her neck. She turned around to see his smiling face.

"Hi, beautiful," he said. "That bathing suit is awesome. Or I guess I should say you look awesome in it."

"Thanks," Emma said, blushing happily.

Kurt took Emma's hand and they headed for the shallow end. A water volleyball game was just getting organized, so they sat on the steps with their ankles in the water.

"I've been thinking about you a lot," Kurt said in a low voice.

"I've been thinking about you, too," Emma admitted.

"Well, that's good." Kurt grinned. "Unrequited love is a bitch!"

Emma smiled back. *Did he actually say the 'L' word?? It's just an expression*, she told herself. *No one talks about unrequited 'like'*.

"Excuse me for interrupting, guys," said Sam, plopping down next to Emma, "but has anyone seen my alleged date?"

Kurt looked uncomfortable. "I haven't seen Kip."

Sam sighed and stood up. "It's already an hour later than I said I'd meet him. Maybe I'll go inside and check the buffet. See ya."

"He wouldn't stand her up, would he?" Emma asked Kurt.

"Don't ask me," Kurt said, looking down.

"Why do I have the feeling you know more than you're telling?" Emma asked.

"Let's just say that I wouldn't put it past Kip."

"Well, if he was going to stand her up, why would he ask her out in the first place?" Emma asked.

Kurt sighed. "Look, the guy is a first-class jerk, if you want to know the truth. I happen to know he's got it bad for Ginny Leighton—"

"The lifeguard?" Emma asked.

"Right," Kurt said. "And Ginny won't give him the time of day. But Ginny told me she was all bummed out because she couldn't come to the party, she has to baby-sit, so . . ."

"So you think maybe Kip went over there to console her?" Emma asked him.

"I don't like spreading rumors, Emma, even about lowlifes like Kip."

Emma looked over at Sam wandering around by herself. "Even if the rumor is probably true," she said.

Kurt just shrugged.

"This is horrible!" Emma said. "Everyone's going to know Kip stood her up."

"I agree with you, it is horrible." Kurt said.

"Like I said, the guy's a lowlife. Man, if there's one thing I can't stand it's insincerity."

"Me, too!" Emma agreed passionately. But then she had to turn her face away from Kurt, because it suddenly occurred to her that she was being awfully hypocritical. *No*, Emma told herself. *I'm nothing like Kip. I'm not an insincere liar. Just because I'm not telling Kurt every little thing about my life does not make me a liar. It makes me . . . mysterious.*

"Hey, want to get into this volleyball game?" Kurt asked.

"I'm afraid I won't be very good at this," said Emma, who had never played any kind of volleyball in her life.

"Doesn't matter," said Kurt. "Come on, it's fun."

And it was. As soon as Emma got the hang of hitting the ball up into the air, it really wasn't very difficult. Their team won the first game and lost the second. The third game was neck and neck, until finally their team needed only one more point to win. The ball was spiked to Emma. She did a setup, bumping the ball to Kurt, who spiked it over the net.

"We won!" Emma screamed, throwing her arms in the air.

"The champ!" Kurt cried, hugging Emma and laughing with her. Emma felt Kurt's hard body pressed up against hers and the laughter stopped. She looked up into his eyes as he pressed her close and kissed her gently.

109

"Let's go for a walk," Kurt said in a husky voice.

Emma nodded. Kurt picked up two of the fluffy terry-cloth robes that the club provided to guests, and they strolled hand in hand through the club to the deserted back porch.

Emma shivered as a night breeze hit her.

"Here," Kurt said, helping her into the robe. "This'll help." He rubbed her back and arms through the robe. "Better?"

Emma smiled up at him. "Are you always this nice?"

"Try asking my sisters what I'm like first thing in the morning." Kurt laughed, hugging Emma.

Emma was quiet for a moment. "You seem to have your life so . . . together," Emma said softly.

"Oh, sure." Kurt laughed again.

"No, I mean it," Emma insisted. "I guess I envy you, in a way."

"Hey, Emma, everyone's got their hassles. Believe me, I've got mine, too. I just don't believe in hanging them out on a line for the world to see."

"Yes, well, that's exactly the sort of thing I mean," Emma said earnestly. "You have . . . character."

"Whatever that means."

"It means you know what you want and you go for it," Emma said.

Kurt pulled Emma to him. "What I want, Emma Cresswell, is you." He kissed her lightly, then more passionately. Slowly he drew the robe away from one shoulder, and lightly kissed down her neck to her shoulder. The he returned to her mouth. Emma felt breathless, as if the room were spinning. It was wonderful, exquisite, and scary, all at the same time. When Kurt moved to caress her breasts, she moved away from him.

"Wait, I . . . I . . . ," she stammered.

"I'm sorry, Emma. You don't need to say anything. I was going too fast."

"I . . . don't have much experience at this, to tell you the truth," she said with a shaky little laugh. "I haven't dated much."

"That's hard to believe, Emma. You're so beautiful," Kurt said.

"Actually, I've had the same boyfriend forever—"

"So there's another guy?" Kurt asked in a steely tone of voice.

"No, no, it's not like that," Emma hastened to explain. "Trent is my mother's best friend's son. We just always got sort of thrown together. I like him, but more like a friend."

"Is this Trent guy still in the picture?" Kurt asked Emma.

"No," Emma said, biting her lower lip. That wasn't exactly true. She hadn't told Trent she wasn't going to see him anymore. *But I will*, Emma told herself.

"You broke up with him?"

"Yes," Emma said. How could she explain that

as far as she was concerned he'd never really been in the picture to begin with?

Kurt took Emma gently into his arms. "Emma, I really care about you."

"I care about you, too," Emma said softly.

Kurt kissed her again. The melting feeling came over her again.

"Whoa, Ackerman, nice form," called a masculine voice. Emma looked up to see Kip Prescott's grinning face.

"Seen my date?" he asked Emma easily.

Emma looked at the clock on the wall. Kip was now two and a half hours late for his date with Sam. "Would you excuse me," Emma said to Kurt.

"Sure," said Kurt. "I'll meet you back by the pool."

Emma was too outraged to say anything to Kip. She walked through the club and into the ladies locker room to see if she could find Sam.

And she did find her, sitting on the floor against the wall in the corner, with Carrie sitting next to her.

"Hi," Emma said softly, sliding down the wall to join them. "Kip's here."

Sam laughed a bitter laugh. "Well, isn't that just ducky. Now that he's made me look like a total idiot."

"He didn't make you look like an idiot," Carrie said. "He's the one who looks like a fool."

"Oh yeah, right," Sam said. "Word travels fast around here. I know where he was. He went over to Ginny Leighton's house because she had to baby-sit and couldn't come to the party. He only asked me in the first place because he thought she'd be here and it would make her jealous. I wish I could disappear."

"You could come out and just have fun and ignore him," Carrie suggested.

"That's right," Emma agreed. "If you stay in here he'll know he made you feel bad. Why give him the satisfaction?"

"But everyone has a date," Sam said, pouting.

"You'd be doing me a big favor, believe me." Carrie laughed. "Please, hang out with me and Howie."

"Is he that bad?" Emma asked sympathetically.

"No, that's just the problem," Carrie said. "I'm finding out what a nice guy he is. For example, I found out why he's at a staff party. His college major is special ed, and he's running a program here at the club for kids on the island with learning disabilities. The rich kids' families pay and the poor kids' families don't. And Howie donates all the money to the Special Olympics."

"Howie Lawrence?" Sam asked incredulously. "Dweebie little Howie Lawrence?"

"I'd say dweebie little Howie Lawrence turned out to be much cooler than hunky Kip Prescott," Emma said softly.

"Why are the hot ones always jerks?" Sam sighed.

"Kurt's not," Emma said softly.

"You're right, Em, he's not," Sam said. "Hold

on to that one." Sam took a deep breath and stood up. "Okay," she sighed. "Let's go. I'm going to show Mr. Butthead Prescott that I barely noticed his absence."

Just as they got within sight of the sliding glass doors that separated the pool from the dance floor, Sam stopped. "I can't believe it. Kip's out there slow dancing with some bimbo! He hasn't even given me a thought!" She turned to Carrie. "Let's go find Howie and fight over him."

Carrie laughed and went off with Sam.

"I'm glad that's over," Kurt said, coming up and taking Emma's hand. "Let's dance."

But Emma was rooted to the spot. Out of the men's room and across the floor strode Austin Payne. Right up to a beautiful blonde he grabbed in a passionate clinch.

"I . . . I want to change out of my bathing suit first," Emma said quickly. "I'm a little cold."

"Okay," said Kurt. "Hurry back."

Emma dashed into the women's locker room and tried to think as she changed her clothes. *This is crazy! I can't keep ducking out of parties because of Austin!* She packed her damp bathing suit into her beach bag and tried to figure out what to do. *I'll have to say I'm not feeling well and I want Kurt to take me home.*

Emma headed out of the locker room and steeled herself to lie to Kurt, who was leaning against the wall waiting for her. She took a quick look into the next room and saw Sam dancing with Kip—so much for ignoring him—and the blonde dancing with Austin.

"Kurt, I . . . I'm not feeling very well," Emma said softly.

"Really?" Kurt asked with concern. "Want me to take you home?"

Emma smiled gratefully at Kurt. He was so sweet, such a genuinely good guy. She hated lying to him.

"Would you mind very much?" she asked him.

"No, of course not. Go get your stuff and I'll tell Sam and Carrie. I see Sam's dancing with that jerk Kip."

"Thanks," Emma said quickly. "I'll meet you outside."

"Okay," said Kurt.

Emma went back into the locker room and sat down in front of a long row of mirrors. Her thoughts were racing a million miles an hour. *Why does Austin have to have a show on this island, of all the places in the world?*

Emma got her beach bag and headed out the side door of the club, walking towards the parking lot. In the distance she could see a car starting up, and she knew Kurt was coming around for her. *He is the nicest guy I have ever known*, Emma told herself, *and I'm crazy about him. Please don't let everything get ruined. . . .*

Her thoughts were interrupted by the murmur of low voices ahead of her by the gazebo. As Emma walked toward Kurt's car, she could just barely make out the outline of a man and a woman.

"Yes," she heard the woman breathe, as the man kissed her.

Kurt's car approached, and for a moment his headlights flashed on the couple in the gazebo, now locked in a passionate embrace.

It was the beautiful blonde and Austin Payne. And it was obvious to Emma that his thoughts were far, far away from Emma's mother, the woman he was supposed to love.

NINE

The next morning Jane offered to take Katie to her swimming lesson. For once Emma was glad not to see Kurt. She couldn't very well tell him the truth about what was going on, and she was really tired of lying to him. Frankly, she was tired of lying to everyone.

"Okay, I'm off," Jane said, the car keys in her hand. "You sure you don't mind making the chicken for the picnic tonight?" Jane asked. The Hewitt family and Emma were going to an outdoor concert given by the Portland Symphony Orchestra that evening at Dunes State Park. They'd picnic on the lawn during the concert.

"No, not at all," Emma said vaguely, staring out the window.

"Emma, forgive me if I'm prying," Jane said tentatively, "but you really seem as if you've got something on your mind. Can I help?"

"Oh, no, I'm okay," Emma said listlessly.

Jane stared at Emma a moment, then she smiled. "Okay. But if you ever want to talk, the door is open."

"Thanks, Jane," Emma said with a sigh. *I wish I could tell her*, Emma thought as she took the chicken out of the fridge, *but I just can't. What would I say? "See, Jane, it's like this. I'm rich. I mean I'm really rich, like I have a trust fund in the seven figure range, for example. And did I mention that since I'm an only child I'll be inheriting the family's entire estate, which is worth something like, oh, I don't know, one or two billion, maybe? Of course, none of my friends know about this. Everything I've told them is lies, lies, lies. But now I need someone to talk to because of this little problem with my mother's lecherous, twenty-five-year-old fiancé. . . .'"*

Emma was startled out of her reverie by the ringing of the telephone.

"Hello? I mean, Hewitt residence."

"Hi, Em, it's Carrie."

"Oh, hi, Carrie."

"Gee, you sound terrible. How are you feeling?"

"I'm okay. Maybe I'm just getting a cold."

"Well, that's two parties in a row you've left early. Maybe you ought to stay home and get some rest before you get really sick."

"Maybe," Emma said with a sigh.

"Em? Are you sure you're okay? Did something happen with Kurt?"

"No, no. Kurt's great. I'm just . . . I've got something on my mind."

"Can I help?" Carrie asked kindly.

If you knew the truth about me, you would not

118

be offering to help, Emma thought bitterly to herself.

"No, I have to sort it out myself," Emma said. "Thanks anyway."

"Well, I've got some good news. Claudia just told me Graham and his band are finishing their tour tomorrow. I'm finally going to get to meet him!"

"That's terrific, Carrie," Emma said, mustering up as much enthusiasm as she could.

"I was thinking that maybe if I can take some photos of him, I might be able to sell them," Carrie went on. "So I asked Claudia if it would be all right, and she said she was sure that Graham wouldn't mind. Isn't that great?"

"Yes, it really is. I'm happy for you."

"Something really is wrong," Carrie said. "You can tell me, you know. I'm your friend."

Could she tell Carrie? Emma wanted desperately to tell someone. Maybe Carrie really would understand.

"I've been having this problem," Emma began tentatively.

"Carrie, do you have the car keys?" Emma heard someone call out at the Templeton's house.

"Oopps, I left them in my room," Carrie said. "Hey, Emma? I've got to go. Call me later when we can really talk, okay?"

"Okay," Emma said. But she knew she'd never get up the nerve again.

I know who I can ask for advice! Emma thought suddenly. *Why didn't I think of it before?*

I'll call Aunt Liz. Please be home, she said to herself, as she dialed the long-distance number.

After the third ring, Liz's answering machine came on. "Hi, this is Liz DuMont. I'm in Washington on business until after the 4th of July. Please leave a message after you hear the tone."

Great, Emma thought.

She sat down on her bed, then realized she had sat down on a small box she hadn't noticed when she came in.

"What is this?" Emma said out loud, untying the bedraggled blue ribbon that held the box shut. Inside was a thin gold chain with a tiny heart on it.

It had to be from Ethan. What she couldn't figure out was where he was getting the money to pay for these things. *I don't know how to handle any of this,* Emma thought to herself! *Do I confront him? Tell Jane?* "God, why doesn't life come with an instruction manual?" she asked out loud.

She heard Ethan and Wills come in downstairs, fighting as usual.

"Stinky Stein is not a turd!" Wills yelled back at Ethan.

"Oh yeah? How do you think he got his name?" Ethan asked smugly.

"Hi guys," Emma said, walking into the family room where Wills looked about ready to attack his brother.

"Ethan, could you come help me with the stuff for the picnic tonight?" Emma asked him.

"Sure," Ethan said.

"I think the chicken is done," Emma said, pulling it out of the oven. "What do you think?"

Ethan bent over the chicken. "Yeah, looks done to me."

"I love cold broiled chicken," Emma said. "Your mom's recipe is great."

"It's okay," Ethan said.

Emma started carefully moving the hot chicken to a large platter that she could refrigerate. "I found a present on my bed just now," Emma said casually.

Ethan didn't say anything, he just sat at the table and retied his sneaker.

"It's a beautiful necklace," Emma said. "I was wondering if it was from you."

"Yeah," Ethan said. He studied the floor earnestly.

Emma slid the chicken into the refrigerator and sat down next to Ethan. "Ethan, I really appreciate your gifts. They mean a lot to me. But I'm concerned about where you're getting the money to pay for them."

Ethan finally looked at Emma. "Dad says it's rude to ask the price of a present."

"I wasn't asking the price," Emma explained, "I was asking how you could afford—"

Ethan stood up abruptly, almost knocking over his chair. "You wouldn't ask that if Kurt gave you a present, I bet!"

"No, but that's different," Emma began.

"It is not different. It's exactly the same!"

Ethan yelled. Then he ran out of the kitchen and out the front door.

Well, I really botched that up, Emma thought. *I'm batting exactly zero in every department of my life.*

In the car on the way to the concert that night, Ethan wouldn't even look at Emma. She didn't know what to say or do to make the situation any better. She really did not want to tell his parents—she knew Ethan would feel totally betrayed. Fortunately the Hewitts chalked Ethan's behavior up to just one of his moods. Wills, on the other hand, was his usually sunny, chattering self. It was funny how kids in the same family could be so different, Emma thought.

When they arrived at Dune Park they found a good spot on the grass and set out an old quilt. Just as Emma was unpacking the chicken, Sam wandered over with the twins in tow.

"Hi, Em. I'm glad I ran into you. I wanted to call you today but I didn't get a chance." Sam turned to the twins, who were clad in jeans so tight they looked as if they were spray painted to their legs. "This is a good spot, guys. Spread out the blanket."

"Great!" one of the twins cried, as she dropped her armload of stuff.

"If she's that enthusiastic, there must be cute guys in the vicinity," Sam told Emma.

Sam was right. The twins immediately started

a conversation with two high-school guys sitting on the next blanket.

"Do you or the twins want some chicken?" Jane asked Sam, as she passed out paper plates.

"The twins don't eat in front of boys. It's some kind of weird rule they invented," Sam said, shaking her head. "But I'd love some."

"Sorry I left early last night," Emma said.

"What a fiasco that was," Sam said, biting into a chicken leg. "Mmmm, this is delish!"

"When I left you were actually dancing with Kip Prescott," Emma said, dishing out the potato salad.

"He's a total jerk," Sam said, "but he's a good dancer. How are you feeling, by the way?"

"Better," Emma said.

"You know, you're so lucky to have found Kurt," Sam said between bites. "There are so many scummy, dishonest guys like Kip around, you know?"

The twins started laughing hysterically at something the boys were saying to them. One guy started tickling one of the twins. She shrieked for him to stop, but it was obvious that she loved every minute of it.

Sam turned to the twins. "Hey, the orchestra is tuning up. Maybe you could keep it down to a dull roar, huh?"

"We'll talk more later," Emma promised, as she shoved the used paper plates into a garbage bag.

As the sky grew darker and the music began, Ethan managed to edge closer to Emma. Emma didn't move or say a word. *Oh Ethan,* she thought, *I'm not worthy of your first crush.*

The orchestra was playing Beethoven's Pastorale Symphony, Emma's favorite. She closed her eyes and let the music wash over her. Before she knew it, it was intermission.

"How do you like it so far?" Emma asked Ethan kindly.

"It's great," Ethan said seriously. "I love classical music."

Ethan's parents overheard him and looked at him as if he were crazy. Emma realized he was just saying that to impress her.

"Hey, Emma," Sam said, "isn't that Kurt over there?"

"Where?" Emma asked, getting on her knees so she could see better.

"There," Sam said, pointing to a bench near the orchestra.

"It is Kurt!" Emma said. And Kurt was not alone. Sitting next to him was a girl with long, blond hair held back with a ribbon.

Emma was too shocked to speak.

"Maybe it's not as bad as it looks," Sam said tentatively.

Emma watched as the girl said something to Kurt, and Kurt laughed and put his arm around the girl.

"And maybe it is," Emma whispered. "Oh, Sam, what am I going to do?" she wailed.

Sam gave her a quick hug. "I'm really sorry, Em. Maybe . . . maybe it's just a one-night thing. Did you guys decide that you wouldn't see anyone else?"

"No," Emma admitted, "we didn't. He's free to see anyone he wants. I just didn't think he would," Emma said, trying not to cry.

Ethan patted Emma's arm awkwardly. "It's okay, Emma. He doesn't even deserve you."

Emma tried to smile. "Thanks, Ethan," she managed.

The rest of the concert was ruined for Emma. Every time she looked in Kurt's direction it was like someone was sticking a knife in her heart. A chant kept repeating and repeating itself in her head. *There is no such thing as love, there is no such thing as love. . . .*

When Emma got home she ran upstairs and threw herself on her bed, determined to try to write out her feelings in her journal. The words wouldn't come. *I wish Aunt Liz would call me,* Emma thought miserably. *I even wish I had the kind of mother I could confide in.* But Kat was so distant, for all her pretense at intimacy. *She's still my mother, though,* Emma thought to herself. *I don't want her to find out about Austin the way I just found out about Kurt, and I'm only dating Kurt. Austin is the man she's supposed to marry!* Emma knew what she had to do.

She wiped the tears off her cheeks with the back of her hand, picked up the phone, and dialed her home number.

"Cresswell residence," said Mrs. James in her formal voice.

"Hello, Mrs. James, it's Emma."

"Yes, hello," Mrs. James said.

Gee, don't sound so overjoyed to hear from me, Emma thought. "Is my mother in?"

"Yes, she is. One moment, please."

Emma waited and waited, finally her mother got on the phone.

"Emma dear?"

"Hi, Mother."

"How nice to hear from you! Are you having fun there?"

"I didn't come to have fun, I came to work," Emma said. She winced at the snippiness of her own retort. *Why do I do that?* she asked herself. She took a deep breath. "I am having fun, mother. The island is lovely."

"Good, dear," her mother said.

"Uh, Mom, did you know that Austin is having a show at a gallery here?"

"He is?" Kat said, sounding totally surprised.

"Oh, I guess you didn't know," Emma said. "I thought maybe that was why you were planning to come here."

"Well, it must be a very small show, darling," Kat said. "I'd know about anything important."

"Yes, well, I guess it is a small show," Emma said.

"Have you seen him?" Kat asked her daughter.

"I keep missing him," Emma lied.

"Oh, well, this will work out splendidly then! I can surprise him when I come to visit the Arpells!" Kat said. "When is the show?"

"It's Saturday night," Emma said. "But mother—"

"We'll have such fun!" Kat interrupted. "Do you think I should bring the green Boulez sheath or the black Lucienne mini for the opening?"

"I . . . I don't think you should come for the opening, mother," Emma said. "I mean, a surprise might not be such a good idea."

Kat laughed a brittle laugh into the phone. "Oh, nonsense, Emma. I know Austin just a little better than you do. He loves surprises!"

Emma clutched the phone cord so hard that her knuckles turned white. "It's just that"—she took a deep breath—"he's seeing someone else."

There was silence on the other side of the phone.

"Mother?" Emma finally said. "Are you there?"

"Why do you say such things, Emma?" Kat asked softly. "You must really hate me."

"No! No, I don't hate you! I saw him—"

"Why do you do this, then?" Kat demanded.

"I saw him kissing another woman!" Emma screamed. "At a party!"

"Stop it, Emma!" her mother commanded. "It isn't true and you know it."

"It is true!" Emma cried.

"Emma, I've known for some time that you are jealous of my relationship with Austin, but I am sickened that you'd stoop to this."

Hot tears came to Emma's eyes.

"I don't know why you want to hurt me this badly, Emma," her mother said. "I really don't."

"But mother I—"

"I can't talk to you anymore." Kat choked back a sob.

"Mother!" Emma yelled. But no one was there. Her mother had hung up on her.

Emma slammed the receiver down and threw herself down on her bed. She felt totally alone.

"Oh please someone, anyone, please . . ." Emma whispered.

But there was no answer.

TEN

The next day at Katie's swimming lesson, Emma dressed in old jeans and a T-shirt, and she stayed far away from Kurt. *I refuse to try to impress him*, she thought as she chose her clothes. *If he wants to go out with someone else, fine. If he's just playing games with me, fine.*

Emma sat down in a beach chair as far from the pool as possible. When Kurt tried to catch her eye, she put on a pair of dark sunglasses. *I was such a little idiot*, Emma ranted to herself. *My mother is crazy about Austin, and look where it got her. So much for honesty and caring and feeling vulnerable. I won't make that mistake again.*

"Emma, can we sit closer to the pool?" Katie asked her tentatively.

"Maybe you feel ready to go join the other kids," Emma suggested. She didn't want Katie to suffer just because Kurt had turned out to be two-timing her.

"If I go over there, do I have to actually go in the water?" Katie asked anxiously.

"No, sweetie," Emma said, giving Katie a hug.

"Just like Kurt said. He made you a promise, remember?"

Katie nodded solemnly. *Right*, Emma thought. *So much for truth, justice, and the American way. Let's just hope Kurt is a bit more straightforward with three-year-old females than he is with eighteen-year-olds.*

"Okay," Katie said, "but I'm not getting wet."

"That's fine," Emma assured her.

"Sally says she wants to stay with you," Katie said, putting the doll on the chair next to Emma.

Emma watched as Katie tentatively walked over to the group of children. She saw Kurt smile at Katie, but he didn't make a big deal out of her joining the group.

So he's good with kids, so what? Emma asked herself. She pulled out a book and started to read. *This is how interested I am in looking at you, Kurt Ackerman.*

When the lesson was finished, Kurt walked over to Emma, moved Sally from the next chair, and sat down.

"Hi," he said.

Emma didn't put down her book. "Hello," she said coolly.

"I don't have to be a mind reader to figure out that something is bothering you," Kurt said.

"Emma, can I go talk to my friend Jessica?" Katie asked, pointing to a chubby girl with blond curls standing with her mother by the pool.

"Yes, but walk, don't run," Emma said automatically.

"Emma? What's up?" Kurt asked.

"Nothing's up," Emma said stiffly. She put down the book but she still refused to look at Kurt.

"Could you take off those stupid sunglasses so I can talk to you?" Kurt asked her.

"No. I like my stupid sunglasses."

Kurt shook his head and ran one hand through his hair in exasperation. "Am I missing something here? A couple of nights ago we went to a party together. I thought we had a great time. You thought you were getting a cold so we left early, and that's the last time I saw you, so what's the deal?"

"Well, that's not the last time I saw you!" Emma blurted out before she could stop herself.

"What are you talking about? And take off those stupid glasses so I can see you!" Kurt said, lifting them off Emma's face before she could stop him.

Emma forced herself to look Kurt straight in the eye. "For a guy who knows all about honesty, you neglected to mention to me that you're dating someone else."

"Excuse me?" Kurt asked.

"Not that it matters," Emma added hastily. "It's not like we ever said we wouldn't see anyone else or even couldn't see anyone else—"

"Emma," he said softly. "What are you talking about?"

Emma willed herself not to cry. "I saw you,"

she whispered, "at the concert last night with that blonde—"

Kurt looked surprised for an instant, and then he laughed. "Emma, that blonde you saw me with is my sister Faith. She's a junior in high school and she plays the flute, so she asked me to take her to the concert."

Emma could feel the color rising in her face. "I feel like a total idiot."

"Oh Kurt! Kurt!" one of the Jacobs twins yelled, running over to him. "Can you check out my form on a dive?"

"I'm busy now, Allie," Kurt said. "I'll show you later."

"I'm Becky," she said, and pouted, "and you don't look so busy to me."

"Emma, can I go to Jessica's for lunch?" Katie asked, pulling on Emma's T-shirt for attention. "I been invited."

Jessica's mom walked over with her little girl in tow.

"Hi, I'm Helaine Ridgewood."

"Emma Cresswell," Emma said, shaking the older woman's hand. *God, I'm supposed to be working here, and all I'm thinking about is Kurt.*

"Yes, I know who you are. Katie talks about you all the time. Jessica has invited Katie for lunch and a play date, if that's all right."

"Yes, I think it's fine. I'll tell Jane. What time should I pick Katie up?"

"Oh, I'll drop her home before dinner," Helaine said.

Emma hugged Katie. "Be a good girl, sweetie," she said, as the little girl toddled off with her friend.

"Look, Emma," Kurt said when they were finally alone again. "Why didn't you just come over and say hello instead of jumping to conclusions?"

"Hey, Kurt, can I show you my new dive?" one of the twins asked.

Kurt groaned in exasperation. "I just told you I was busy!"

The girl looked hurt. "That wasn't me. It must have been Becky."

"Later," Kurt said to her tersely. "Look, I don't have another lesson for two hours," Kurt told Emma, "the kids are just used to my hanging around to help them. Let's get out of here, okay?"

Emma nodded yes and they went out to Kurt's car. He drove in silence to the dunes, parked the car, and the two of them went walking on the beach.

For quite a while neither of them said anything. Emma couldn't think of a thing to say that didn't sound ridiculous. Finally they stopped walking at a deserted spot and sat down in the sand, staring out at the water.

"Why didn't you just ask me?" Kurt said softly.

"How could I?" Emma said. "It's not like we've ever discussed it. I didn't have any right—"

"But you do have the right," Kurt corrected her. "Hey, I'd be ticked if I thought you were out with someone else."

"You would?" Emma asked, digging her toes in the sand.

"Emma, when I say I care, I meant it. And I can't care about two girls at once."

"You could if you wanted to," Emma said in a small voice. She wanted Kurt's reassurance, but at the same time it scared her. She remembered the refrain going through her head only the night before: *there is no such thing as love. . . .*

"No, I couldn't," Kurt said firmly. "I think that's a lot of crap people say because they're afraid of commitment. I don't want to see anyone but you."

"Oh, that's how I feel, too," Emma whispered fervently. Kurt put his arms around her and kissed her lightly, then more urgently. The feeling of the sun on her face and Kurt's mouth on hers made her feel warm and safe and excited all at the same time. The next thing Emma knew she was lying on her back in the sand, Kurt lying half over her, kissing her passionately.

Emma's entire body felt like an electric current was running through it. It felt exquisite, and it also felt dangerous, almost out of control.

"Stop, please," Emma said holding one hand up to Kurt's chest. He rolled over onto his back with a groan and threw his hand over his face. Finally he chuckled. "You're right. This is not exactly the time or the place."

Emma sat up. "I'm not used to this, Kurt. It . . . it scares me."

"Hey, it's okay, really!" Kurt said. "I honestly

don't mean to rush you. We'll take things how ever you feel comfortable."

"What if I'm not ready to take things at all?" Emma asked anxiously.

"You mean have sex?" Kurt asked.

Emma nodded.

"Emma, you can call the shots on that, okay? I promise."

"Really? You won't get mad?"

"Emma, I told you, I care about you. Sure, I'm incredibly attracted to you, but I'm in no rush."

"You're sure?" Emma asked.

"Look, I can't tell you it's always going to be easy." Kurt laughed a little. "But I can handle it. The only thing I can't handle is if you play games with me or lie to me."

At that moment Emma wanted to tell Kurt the entire truth about herself more than she wanted anything in the world. *He really cares about me, and he'll understand*, she thought.

"I . . . I . . . there's something I need to tell you," Emma began. Her hands were shaking, and she could feel her heart beating double time in her chest.

Kurt looked at his watch. "I've got to give a private lesson to Alexa Pope at three o'clock. The poor kid is a really pathetic case," Kurt said. "Her parents think that their money can buy their little overprivileged darling anything, including friendship. They're really just paying me to pay attention to her. Anyway, what did you want to tell me?"

135

No! I can't tell him! Kurt thinks rich people are pampered snobs who take everything for granted. And I suppose I was like that a little, but I'm changing! I'm changing, and there's no one I can tell. . . .

"Emma? What did you want to tell me?" Kurt repeated.

"Oh, it's . . . um . . . about Ethan. It, um, seems he's developed a crush on me."

"He's got good taste," Kurt said.

"Well, he's been giving me expensive gifts. A scarf, a necklace . . ."

"Where does he get the money for that?" Kurt asked.

"That's what I can't figure out. The wrapping job looks like he's doing it himself. But the gifts are brand-new. I'm afraid he's stealing, either from a store or from someone."

"Did you ask him?"

"Yes, but he was just evasive."

"In other words, he's lying to you without actually lying to you," Kurt said.

"Something like that."

"Well, it's a tough one," Kurt said. "I'm sure you don't want to tell his parents. The kid would be mortified. Would you like me to talk to him?"

"Bad idea," Emma said. "He considers you the enemy because I'm dating you."

Kurt pulled Emma close. "So my competition is an eleven-year-old?"

"At the moment you have no competition," Emma whispered, and kissed Kurt passionately.

She wanted to forget everything, all the evasions and lies she had told, and just lose herself in this wonderful new feeling.

But too soon they had to drive back to the club so that Kurt could meet Alexa. In the car all the terrible anxieties washed over Emma once again. *All right, so I'll just enjoy this for as long as it lasts, then. Tomorrow will have to take care of itself.*

"The Hewitts are having a big party Friday night," Emma said. "Would you like to come?"

"I'm driving the hack until ten, but I could come after that," Kurt offered.

"Great," Emma said, smiling at Kurt. Fortunately he was too busy driving to see that the smile never reached her eyes.

ELEVEN

Thursday morning dawned bright, sunny, and perfect. Emma, Carrie, and Sam all had the morning off and had planned to meet on the boardwalk at ten o'clock.

Carrie had already arrived and was sitting on a bench in front of the arcade, her face held up to the sun.

"Hi," said Emma, sitting down next to her on the bench.

"Hi," Carrie answered, not moving her face. "Isn't it a glorious day? Why does the sun feel so much better here than it does in New Jersey?"

"Maybe it's magic," Emma said, pulling her knees up to her chin.

"Hey, tomorrow's the big day," Carrie said. "Claudia is meeting Graham's plane in Portland at two o'clock. I'm actually going to meet him!"

"You're actually going to live with him," Emma said with a laugh, "which is even better."

"Live in the same house, anyway," Carrie corrected. "I have to admit I'm really excited about this. I wrote Josh and told him, now he's begging for an invitation to Sunset Island."

"I thought you and Josh broke up," Emma said.

139

She reached into her beach bag and got out the sunblock.

"We did," Carrie sighed. "I don't know. I'm confused."

"Well, join the club," Emma said, as she rubbed sunblock into her legs.

"What are you confused about?" Carrie asked her. "I thought you and Kurt were crazy about each other."

"We are, it's just complicated," Emma said.

"Hey, aren't you that world-famous photographer Carrie Alden?" Sam asked as she strode up to them. "And aren't you Emma Cresswell, princess of a small Nordic nation?"

"Please, no autographs," Carrie said, waving her hand at Sam.

"We're traveling incognito," Emma added.

"Is today gorgeous or is today gorgeous?" Sam asked as she joined them on the bench. "Mmmmm, I smell caramel corn," she added, sniffing the air. "Let's go get some."

"It's ten-thirty in the morning," Emma pointed out.

"Let me ask you a question," Sam said, standing up. "Do you think your stomach knows what time it is and will reject anything but breakfast food?"

"I haven't even had tea yet," Emma objected.

"Oh, tea?" Sam said in a teasing voice, pulling Emma and Carrie to their feet. "How could this happen? Didn't Reginald serve you in bed upon your awakening? How lax of him! I'll have him drawn and quartered, or quartered and drawn, or something."

"I think caramel corn for breakfast is an excellent idea," Carrie said, "it's my hips that don't."

"Where did I find you spoilsports?" Sam asked, pushing them toward the caramel corn stand in the arcade.

"It smells heavenly," Carrie admitted, inhaling deeply.

"Three caramel corns, please," Sam ordered from the young girl behind the bright red cart.

"What size?" the girl asked.

"Small!" Carrie and Emma said at the same time.

"Two small, one large," Sam ordered.

The three girls strolled down the boardwalk, chomping happily on the hot caramel corn.

"I saw Kurt yesterday at the club," Sam said. "He kept talking about you, Miss Emma, so that other girl he was out with must not be very important."

Carrie looked at Emma. "Kurt was out with another girl!?"

"Believe it or not, that 'other girl' was his sister," Emma said with a wry smile.

"His sister?" Sam repeated. "Oh, Em, that's great! I'm so happy for you!"

"Thanks," Emma said. "I felt like a total idiot when he told me."

"So why aren't you exuberant? Jumping for joy, etcetera, etcetera?" Sam demanded.

Emma shrugged. "I just have a lot on my mind,

I guess," she said softly. "Oh, I meant to tell you two, the Hewitts are having a huge party tomorrow night, to which you are both invited."

"Sounds great," Carrie said.

"Yeah, any place I can go without the monsters is a place I want to be," Sam said. "Do we bring dates?"

"If you want," Emma said. "I invited Kurt."

"Well, Carrie, I definitely think you should invite Howie Lawrence," Sam said, licking caramel off a finger.

"Hey, don't rag on Howie," Carrie said, "He happens to be a great guy. There's just no chemistry, you know what I mean?"

"In other words, he doesn't make you want to drop your drawers," Sam said.

"She's such a colorful girl, isn't she, Emma?" Carrie giggled.

"Hey, look over there," Sam said, nudging Emma in the ribs. She was pointing to a store called Wheels. Outside the store were bicycles, mopeds, and motorcycles for rent by the hour, and leaning against the sign giving rental information was a tall, blond-haired guy in cutoffs and a muscle shirt.

"What do you have, some kind of man radar?" Carrie asked Sam.

"He's very handsome," Emma said. "Do you know who he is?"

"When a guy is that cute I make it my business to know who he is. He manages Wheels and his name is Presley."

"As in Elvis?" Carrie asked, making a face.

Sam shrugged. "I don't know. Let's go ask him." Sam stuffed their caramel corn bags in the nearest trash can and made a beeline for Wheels.

"Hi, there," Sam said when they reached the store. "My friend here would like to know if you were named after Elvis Presley." Sam indicated Carrie with a nod of her head.

How does she do this kind of thing so easily? Emma wondered for the hundredth time. *Even Carrie looks comfortable. And me, even if I was absolutely dying to meet him, I'd probably wait until we were introduced by mutual friends.*

Presley shielded his eyes from the glare of the sun to get a better look at the girls. "She does, huh?" Presley asked Sam in a teasing voice. "But you don't?"

"Oh, maybe a little," Sam admitted with a grin.

Emma bit her lip so she wouldn't laugh. It seemed that Sam was being outflirted!

"Hey, Pres, we got time to stop at the camera shop before we go?" a guy asked, coming out of Wheels. He was wearing torn, faded jeans and a navy T-shirt that he filled out to perfection. His streaky blond hair was tied back with a piece of rawhide, and he had a tiny diamond stud in one ear. He was fiddling around with a camera that was strung around his neck.

"I know you," Sam said. "You're Billy . . . something or other. You were at Howie Lawrence's party the other night, right?"

"Sure was. Fun party, huh?" Billy asked.

"Hey, that's a Canon EOS, isn't it?" Carrie asked, pointing to the camera.

"Yeah, it is," Billy said. "I just got it."

"It's beautiful," Carrie breathed. "I've been wanting one but . . . could I take a look at it?"

"Sure," Billy said easily, slipping the camera off his neck. "You a photographer?"

"I try," Carrie said, examining the camera. "This is awesome. . . ."

"She won second prize in a New Jersey state competition," Emma said in her quiet voice. "She's really very talented."

"Yeah?" Billy said appreciatively. "Maybe you could give me some pointers, then. I'm just getting started with it."

"Right!" said Sam, snapping her fingers. She looked at Billy. "You sing with Flirting with Danger, right? Your demo tape was playing at the party!"

"Sure do," Billy said, "and Pres here plays bass."

"The tape we heard was wonderful," Emma said sincerely.

Sam looked at Pres. "So, let's see, you're a musician, and you've got some kind of southern accent—"

"Tennessee," Pres said with a grin.

"Tennessee accent." Sam nodded. "So I guess that means you really were named after Elvis!"

"You got me," Pres said.

Carrie was still mesmerized by Billy's camera.

"I've read the instant override on this is unbelievable," Carrie said.

"Yeah, it's great for speed shots," Billy said. "The self-focus is so good that the camera reacts as if you'd had, like, five minutes to set up the shot!"

"That's what I heard," Carrie said, nodding. "I'd love to try it sometime," she said, wistfully turning the camera over in her hands.

"Maybe we could work something out," Billy said. "For sure you know more about using it than I do."

"Hey, I hate to interrupt you two, but we gotta boogie," Presley told Billy. "I left Dustin in charge of the store, but I've still got to get back here in time to close up."

"Oh, sorry," Carrie said hastily, handing the camera back to Billy. "I didn't mean to keep you."

"Hey, no problem," Billy said. "I really would love to talk to you about it some more sometime. What's your name?"

"Carrie Alden."

"You live on the island?"

"Work," Carrie corrected. "I'm an au pair for the Templetons."

Billy's face lit up. "You mean Graham and Claudia, right?"

"You know them?" Carrie asked.

"Sure. Graham's great, what a musician," Billy said appreciatively.

"I haven't met him yet," Carrie explained. "He's getting home tomorrow."

"Yeah, he talked to us about maybe opening for them on a local gig," Pres said. "It would be a big break for us."

"Well, I'm sure I'll see you around, then," Billy said to Carrie. He took her hand and held it a moment. "It was really nice to meet you," he said warmly.

"You, too," Carrie said.

"Come on, lover boy," Pres said good-naturedly as he pulled Billy away from Carrie. Then he winked at Sam. "Stay sweet," he said, as the two walked away down the boardwalk.

"I'm in love," Sam said, as they watched the guys walk away.

"Yeah, Billy really is cute," Carrie said.

"Not Billy! Presley!" Sam corrected her. "Did you hear that voice? I can just imagine him whispering dirty words in my ear."

"We should keep her locked up for her own good!" Emma laughed.

"Do you think he liked me?" Sam asked her friends.

"How could he help himself?" Emma said loyally.

"I thought you were crazy for that artist, Austin Payne?" Carrie asked in a teasing voice.

"Austin Payne doesn't have that voice," Sam sighed dreamily. "Anyway, you know me," Sam said, "I've got a short attention span. Austin told me at the staff party that he was leaving the island until his opening, which isn't until Saturday night."

"Out of sight, out of mind," Carrie teased her.

"Not to mention that he's with a different babe every time I see him," Sam said.

"Yeah, you're the only one whose supposed to be able to get away with that kind of behavior!" Carrie said.

"Why don't we rent some bikes as long as we're here?" Emma suggested. Although she was relieved to know she didn't have to worry about running into Austin until Saturday, she definitely did not want to have a conversation about his prowess as a ladies' man.

"Yeah, let's," Carrie said.

They went inside and arranged to have three bikes for two hours.

"Let's bike out to the far pier," Carrie suggested.

It felt wonderful biking down the boardwalk with the breeze blowing back their hair. When they got to the pier, they parked their bikes and sat on one of the benches.

"I love it here," Emma said quietly, staring out at the aqua blue water.

"Me, too," Sam agreed in a soft voice. "Kansas seems very far away."

"Kansas *is* very far away," Carrie said, laughing, "but I know what you mean. Like the fall, going back to school, all the decisions and hassles. . . ."

"Sometimes I feel like I'd like to stay here forever," Emma sighed.

The girls sat staring out over the water. A gull

swooped down and caught a fish in its beak, then soared through the sky again.

"Sometimes I feel like that fish," Sam blurted out. Her friends looked at her. "Like something bigger than me is carrying me away."

"I think I know what you mean." Emma nodded.

"Like going to Kansas State, for example," Sam said. "I don't know if I want to go there. But I got this dance scholarship, and it's what my family can afford. It's like . . . I don't have a chance to figure out what I really want, you know?"

"I *do* know!" Emma said passionately. "Everyone just assumes I'll go to Ballantrae College, because it's where my mother went and where her mother went. They just assume I'll be a French major, just like my mother was. But I already speak fluent French, I've already read all the classics in French—"

"You've read all the classics in French?" Carrie asked her. "That's incredible! Were you an exchange student or something?"

This is it, Emma thought. *This is my chance to tell them the truth. They'll understand, because they really care about me.*

"No," Emma began in a small voice. "Actually—"

"It just isn't fair that my options are limited because my family doesn't have money!" Sam interrupted. "The rich kids on this island don't have a clue. They can do whatever they want, and they don't even appreciate it. It sucks."

"Come on," Carrie chided, "we've got it better than the majority of the world, and we should appreciate that. Anyway, what were you saying, Em?"

"Nothing," Emma said softly. "It wasn't important."

"Let's take the bike path around to the bay side," Carrie suggested, getting up to stretch. "We can go the long way around the island and still get the bikes back in time."

They rode their bikes in silence for a while, enjoying the sun and the sweet air. When they reached the bay side, Carrie pulled her bike up in front of the Sunset Art Gallery.

"Let's stop in a sec," Carrie suggested.

"Okay," Emma said easily, thankful that she knew she couldn't possible run into Austin.

They parked their bikes and walked inside to the coolness of the gallery.

"Come on, Em, I'll show you Kishouru Mobishi's photos," Carrie said, leading them through a small exhibit to the larger main room of the gallery.

"Oh, wonderful, Lorell is here," Sam muttered sarcastically under her breath.

Lorell was with Daphne and another girl. They were standing in front of the photo of Austin Payne that hung by his paintings.

Emma knew the other girl. She knew the other girl well. It was Diana De Witt, the most obnoxious, most superficial, most hateful girl in the entire graduating class at Aubergame, Emma's Swiss boarding school.

"Why Emma Cresswell," Diana purred, "as I live and breathe."

There was no place Emma could go, no place to hide. She just stood there, mute, like a butterfly captured under a pin. Carrie and Sam looked at Emma, waiting to find out who this new girl was.

"This is just such a coincidence!" Diana continued in her fake voice. She tapped one perfectly manicured finger on Austin Payne's photograph. "Imagine running into you, and an exhibit by your mother's boy-toy, all in the same afternoon!"

Lorell and Daphne grinned maliciously. Sam and Carrie just looked confused.

"Austin Payne?" Sam asked. "Her mother's what?"

"Didn't Emma tell you?" Diana asked innocently.

"Emma's mother, who happens to be one of the richest heiresses in America, supports Austin Payne in a style to which he would like to become accustomed. In other words"—she grinned sweetly—"they're engaged."

TWELVE

"They're what?" Carrie asked, not sure that she had heard correctly.

"Engaged," Diana repeated sweetly. "You know, as in going to be married."

"I just hope that your daddy-dearest-to-be signed a prenuptial agreement with your momma," Lorell said, all full of concern. "You don't think he could be after her money, do you?"

"Oh, perish the thought!" Diana cried.

Sam turned to Emma. "This is some kind of joke, right?"

Everyone in the room stared at Emma, waiting for her response. But what could she say? Where could she begin? She only wished that a huge hole in the floor would open underneath her and she could fall in and sink out of sight and never have to face any of them again.

"I . . . I . . . ," Emma began.

"Oh, I'm being so rude!" Diana trilled. "I haven't even introduced myself. I'm Diana De Witt. I went to boarding school with Emma. In Switzerland. Well, there was that one semester we all spent in Paris, but I'm sure Emma's told you all about that."

Lorell wagged a finger at Emma. "It was just so naughty that you lied to me! I mean, about being one of *the* Cresswells. I could tell just by looking at you that you weren't really one of *them*," Lorell said derisively, cocking her head in Sam and Carrie's direction. Sam's face turned as pale as the whitewashed stucco walls of the gallery.

"I decided to check with Daddy," Lorell continued, "and he called the De Witts in Boston. I've known Diana forever. Our families have beach houses right near each other in the south of France."

"When Lorell called me and told me you were working—working!—on Sunset Island and pretending to be poor, I thought it was one of the funniest things I'd ever heard in my life," Diana continued. "I told Lorell I just had to come for a visit and see it for myself. I said 'Imagine Emma Alexandra Cresswell, the biggest snob at Aubergame Academy, putting one over on everyone. It's too hilarious!'"

Daphne laughed a brittle laugh and pushed her hair behind her ear with a shaky hand. "Lorell, Emma's family is actually much richer than yours."

Lorell pursed her lips. "And of course that means they're richer than yours, too."

Sam and Carrie just looked from Emma to Lorell and back to Emma. "Let's get out of here," Sam finally said through clenched teeth.

Emma turned and ran toward the door of the

gallery. Sam and Carrie followed her, but not before all three could hear Diana's parting shot.

"Have fun slumming!" she called. The laughter of Diana and Lorell and Daphne echoed through the gallery.

When Emma reached the front of the gallery, she grabbed on to a pillar to keep from falling over. She felt like she was going to throw up or faint. She leaned her head against the pillar and took gulps of air.

"What the hell is going on here?" Sam demanded.

"Hey, take it easy," Carrie said, putting a restraining hand on Sam's arm. "Give Emma a chance to explain."

"Okay," Sam said, crossing her arms, "we'll give Emma a chance to explain. So go ahead," she demanded, "explain."

"It's . . . it's . . . difficult to explain," Emma said in a tortured voice.

"Oh, but it wasn't difficult to lie to us," Sam shot back.

"I didn't exactly lie to you," Emma said in a shaky voice, "I just never mentioned that my family is wealthy. Why should it matter?"

Even Carrie had to shake her head at that. "Emma, if it didn't matter you wouldn't have felt like you had to lie about it."

Emma looked at the toes of her sneakers. To her mortification the view began to blur as tears welled up in her eyes. "I just wanted to be treated like everyone else," she whispered.

"That is the biggest crock I ever heard!" Sam stormed. "God, you must have been laughing at me all the time, going on about rich people this and rich people that. What did you do, call home and laugh at me with all your rich friends?"

"Oh, no!" Emma cried. "That's just the whole point! I didn't want to be like them! I can't stand all of that! And I can't stand Diana! I . . . I wanted to just be accepted for who I am."

"Well, who the hell is that?" Sam screamed.

Emma couldn't look at Sam's angry, betrayed face. She looked at Carrie, hoping she would understand.

"Carrie?"

Carrie shook her head. "You never gave us a chance to even know who you are," Carrie said sadly. "You never gave us a chance at all."

Sam folded her arms and stared hard at Emma. "And what's this about Austin Payne?" she demanded. "You mean to tell me your mother is engaged to Austin Payne?"

"Yes, but—"

"Unbelievable!" Sam yelled. "You let me go on and on about him. You let me make a total fool of myself!"

"He's the fool!" Emma cried. "He's just a lying little cheat—"

"Well, if that isn't the pot calling the kettle black," Sam sneered.

"Look, we've got to get the bikes back," Carrie said in a low tone. "I think we should chill out and talk about this later when everyone isn't feeling so hurt."

Sam marched over to her bike and viciously kicked the kickstand up. "Fine, Carrie. You can be Little Miss Maturity. I, for one, have absolutely nothing to say to Emma. Ever again." Sam got on her bike and pedaled away.

Carrie and Emma walked over to their bikes. Carrie looked at Emma. "You really hurt her," Carrie said.

"I didn't mean to."

"But you did it, anyway! I don't know, maybe you're so rich you think that you can just do or say whatever you want—"

"Oh, no, Carrie, please don't think that—"

"I don't know what to think," Carrie said, getting on her bike. "Listen, I want to ride by myself. I need to be alone for awhile."

"But I have to take my bike back, too," Emma said in a small voice.

"Take it back late," Carrie said, "you can afford the late fee." She pedaled off toward the boardwalk.

Emma watched as Carrie faded to a speck in the distance. Hot tears ran down her cheeks. How could she ever make her friends understand?

When Emma got back to the Hewitts' no one was home. *Good, I don't have to see anyone,* she thought. She threw herself down on her bed. *What am I going to do?* She went to move her pillow under her head, and she felt a small box underneath it.

Oh no, not again, she thought, pulling the box out. She took off the clumsily wrapped box and saw a small bottle of expensive French perfume.

Emma was just so angry at everyone for not understanding why she did what she did. Before she could think about it, she threw the bottle of perfume against the wall with all her might. She missed the wall and hit the drapes next to the window. The bottle fell from the drapes onto the cushions in front of the window seat.

"I can't even break a stupid perfume bottle!" she screamed. Then she started to cry, because everything was just so awful. She pulled out her journal and took the pen from her drawer.

Congratulations to me. I've managed to screw up everything. Sam and Carrie hate me. Ethan is stealing gifts for me from who-knows-where, so I'm a failure in that department, too. If it wasn't for Kurt I'd quit my job and run away. It's so unfair. If Sam and Carrie really liked me, they'd try to understand instead of just judging me. If friendship is such a fragile thing, then what is it worth, anyway?

Emma heard footsteps on the stairs, so she quickly stuffed her journal in the drawer on the nightstand, and went into the bathroom to wash her tear-streaked face.

"Emma? You home?" It was Jane's voice at the door.

"Just a second," Emma called, drying her face on a towel. She took a deep breath and went to the door.

"Hi," said Emma, trying to look perky.

"Hi," Jane said tentatively. "You okay?"

"Sure!" Emma said brightly, but she sounded like a fake even to her own ears.

"Can I come in?" Jane asked carefully.

Emma motioned her into the room. Jane sat down on the cushioned window seat and looked down at her hands.

"Emma, I know something is bothering you. I really don't want you to think I'm prying into your life. It's just that . . . well, I'm very fond of you and I hate to see you unhappy."

At the sound of the kindness and concern in Jane's voice, Emma lost it. She sat down on her bed and tears rolled down her cheeks. Jane just sat there patiently, waiting for Emma to talk.

"It's not that awful," Emma said, reaching for a tissue. "I mean, it's not as if someone died or anything."

Jane nodded and waited.

"It's just . . ." Emma twisted the Kleenex into shreds as she tried to find the right words. "I come from a really wealthy family," Emma began slowly. "I didn't need this job. I don't need any job ever in my whole life if I don't feel like working. I . . . didn't want anyone to know, because I thought they'd all treat me differently.

I've never known what it's like to just be a normal person, not 'Emma Cresswell, heiress-to-a-megafortune'. So I didn't tell anyone. Not you, not my friends on the island, not anybody. Well, today this hateful girl from my boarding school showed up here, and she just told my friends everything. And now they hate me. They just think I'm a big liar. They don't understand at all and they won't listen to me." Emma took a big gulp. "I know, I know, everyone in the world would like to have my problems. But I really don't care about the money!" Emma cried passionately. "I feel suffocated by it, can you understand that?"

Jane sighed thoughtfully. "It's easy to say you don't care about money when you have it."

"That's what I mean, no one understands how I feel—," Emma began.

"Wait," Jane said, holding up one hand. "I'm trying to understand. You didn't want your friends here to know because you thought they'd treat you differently, is that right?"

"Yes, that's exactly right!" Emma said.

"Well, I'm not going to lie to you and say that class consciousness doesn't exist," Jane said, "because we both know it does."

Emma nodded.

"It's stupid, of course," Jane continued. "I'd like to think that Jeff and I don't do that—but then of course we aren't that kind of rich."

"But a lot of people on this island *are* that kind of rich," Emma said earnestly. "And they remind me of all the ugly, hypocritical crap I've heard all my life. 'Only have friends who are like us, dear. Only date boys from our class, dear.' Like I could get contaminated by the masses or something!"

"That must be very difficult for you," Jane murmured.

"No, that's just the point," Emma tried to explain. "I didn't even think about it until I was sixteen or seventeen years old. I just swallowed everything my parents told me without thinking about it. I'm just as guilty as they are!"

"No, of course you're not!" Jane said. "Kids believe the things their parents tell them. They don't know any different."

"Well, now I know different," Emma said. "I just want to figure óut what I think, what I believe in—"

"Without the baggage of your parents' values," Jane said, nodding. "I understand."

"Really? Do you really?" Emma asked hopefully.

"I think I do, Emma. I can't tell you I think what you did was right, but I can certainly understand why you did it."

"So why can't my friends understand then?" Emma cried.

"I imagine they're angry. And hurt," Jane said gently.

Emma nodded miserably.

"I think if you give it some time, and if you really try to explain, and if you apologize, they'll forgive you," Jane said.

"Really?" Emma asked hopefully.

"Does Kurt know about all this?"

"I can't tell him," Emma whispered.

"Well, I'd suggest you give that decision some serious thought," Jane said. "You don't want him to find out from someone else, do you?"

"No," Emma said miserably, "but he'll drop me if I tell him."

"Maybe you're underestimating him," Jane said. "You know, your certainty that everyone would have treated you differently—judged you before you had a chance to prove yourself—is just another way of judging people yourself. You came to a lot of unwarranted conclusions, too, Emma. Why don't you give Kurt a chance to accept the real you?"

"Whatever that is," Emma sighed.

Jane smiled and stood to leave: "Well, I suppose this isn't much of a consolation to you, but I think the world of you. And the fact that your family is wealthy has no bearing on that one way or the other."

"Thanks, Jane."

"You're welcome," she said. She crossed the room and closed the door softly behind her.

The phone rang and Emma took a deep breath before answering it.

"Hello?"

"Hi, it's Kurt."

"Oh, hi." Emma's heart beat too rapidly in her chest.

"What's up?" Kurt asked. "You sound funny."

"No, nothing's up," Emma said quickly. Her eyes fell on the forgotten perfume bottle. "Just . . . I got another gift from Ethan."

"The kid's got it bad, huh?" Kurt asked sympathetically.

"I'm not even worth his having a crush on," Emma blurted out.

"Why would you say that?" Kurt asked. "I happen to think you are heavy crush material, myself."

"I'm just feeling sorry for myself," Emma said. "Ignore me."

"Just one of those blue days?"

"I guess so," Emma sighed. She twisted the phone cord around her finger in anxiety. She wanted to confide in Kurt so much, but she just didn't know how to begin!

"Hey, how about the Kurt Ackerman famous cheer-you-up plan?" Kurt asked. "It goes something like this: I come over tonight and pick you up, and we go out to the dunes, where we have a picnic while watching the sunset. What do you think?"

"I think it sounds heavenly," Emma said.

"Great. I'll be by at seven-thirty, okay? And wear that incredible perfume you had on the other day," Kurt added.

"I wasn't wearing perfume," Emma said with surprise.

"I know," Kurt said.

Emma could swear she heard him grinning

through the wire. As she hung up, there was a knock on her door.

"Hey, Em," Ethan called in, "want to play some one-on-one?"

This is my chance, Emma thought. *I've got to get at least one part of my life under control.* She marched purposefully to the door and opened it for Ethan.

"Come on in, Ethan, I want to talk to you," Emma said.

Ethan walked in slowly, carrying his basketball under his arm. He sat down on the bed, so Emma took a seat on the window cushions.

"Maybe you'd like to do something, um, more . . . mature than shoot baskets," Ethan said hopefully.

Emma leaned forward and rested her hands on her knees. "Ethan, I got your present. The perfume."

Ethan shrugged and stared at his basketball.

"I'm flattered—honored—that you would want to give me presents. But I'm really concerned about this," Emma said.

"You wouldn't be concerned if they were from Kurt," Ethan countered.

"The difference is that Kurt works, so if he gave me a gift he would have earned the money to pay for it. I know you don't work, and I can't help but be concerned about how you can afford to give me these gifts," Emma explained.

"Next you're gonna say 'Kurt is a grown-up,

and you're just a stupid little kid,' right?" Ethan asked belligerently.

"I do not think of you as a stupid little kid," Emma said firmly. "But I have a job here. I was hired by your parents to help care for you and your brother and your sister, and this makes me feel like I'm not doing a very good job."

"You're doing a great job, honest!" Ethan said earnestly.

"How good a job can I be doing if you're stealing?"

Ethan examined his basketball again.

"You are stealing, aren't you," Emma said.

"Not exactly," Ethan mumbled.

Emma waited quietly, willing herself to be patient. She didn't feel patient. She felt like everything was out of control and it was her fault. She could hear Wills's voice in the backyard, calling Dog. She could hear the music of an ice cream truck stopping in front of the house.

"I sort of traded stuff," Ethan finally said in a low voice.

"Traded?"

"Yeah, well, see, I had this deal with Stinky."

"Wills's friend Stinky?" Emma asked, completely bewildered.

"Yeah. Because he loves Nintendo," Ethan said.

Emma shook her head. "Ethan, I'm not following this."

Ethan sighed. "See, Stinky's mom, Trina—her own kids actually call her Trina!—well, she's got all this stuff. She never uses it. Stinky says she never even takes it out of the boxes half the time. Stinky's brother Stuey—he's the kid with the braces that I hate—well, Stuey says that his dad buys his mom all this stuff because he feels guilty on account of he's never there."

Emma nodded. She didn't have a clue what Ethan was talking about, but she hoped it would all make sense eventually.

"So," Ethan continued, "I made this deal with Stinky. If he'd get me one good present, I'd give him a Nintendo game. We've got tons of Nintendos and Stinky only has four."

Emma nodded again. It was beginning to make sense.

"So Stinky got me the scarf from his mom," Ethan mumbled, "and I gave it to you."

"And Stinky got you the necklace and the perfume, too?" Emma asked. "And you gave him two more Nintendo games?"

Ethan nodded.

"But that's still stealing," Emma said gently. "The stuff didn't belong to you."

"It's the barter system!" Ethan protested. "We learned about it in history last year."

"You can't barter with what isn't yours, Ethan," Emma rebuked.

Ethan's face was turning redder by the second.

"It seems to me that the truth here is that you stole and you lied," Emma said slowly. "What do you think?"

"I didn't lie," Ethan said, shaking his head. "No way."

"But you did, really. Giving me gifts that were stolen property was a way of lying. Trading Nintendo games that belong to your whole family was a way of lying, too. And when I asked you about where you got the gifts before, you didn't tell me the truth."

"So, I didn't lie, either," Ethan pointed out.

"Not outright, maybe," Emma said, "but doing dishonest things and hiding from the truth are both ways of lying."

Ethan looked over at Emma out of the corner of his eyes. "Are you gonna tell my parents?"

"Are you going to stop stealing Trina Stein's stuff?" Emma countered.

"Yeah."

"And are you going to return everything that you took?"

"Yeah," Ethan agreed.

"And do you promise to stop stealing—or bartering—what doesn't belong to you?" Emma asked.

"I promise," Ethan said.

"Then I promise I won't tell," Emma said. "Now, as long as you keep your promises, I'll keep mine. Do we have a deal?" Emma held out her hand to Ethan.

"Deal," Ethan said, shaking Emma's hand solemnly.

THIRTEEN

Kurt picked Emma up right on time, as usual. He looked gorgeous in a pair of faded jeans, a red T-shirt, and a faded jean jacket. Emma turned on the radio in Kurt's car. A Graham Perry song blasted out. That reminded Emma that Graham was due home the next day, and that reminded her of Carrie and Sam, and *that* reminded her of how they weren't speaking to her and might never speak to her again. She sighed and put her head back on the headrest.

"Whew, some sigh!" Kurt observed. "Want to talk about it?"

"Nothing to talk about," Emma said lightly. "I'm just hungry, I guess."

"Food coming right up," Kurt said.

When they reached the dunes Kurt spread an old quilt on the sand. Then he pulled a picnic hamper out of his trunk. Emma leaned back on her elbows and let the ocean breezes blow gently through her hair.

"I feel better just being here," Emma finally said quietly.

"I'm glad," Kurt said. "I'm sure Rubie's famous

clam chowder will help," he added, unscrewing a thermos.

"Mmm," Emma said, taking a mug from him.

Kurt leaned over and gave her a kiss. "What did you decide to do about Ethan?"

"Actually, I handled it rather well, if I do say so myself," Emma admitted. She told Kurt the entire conversation with Ethan, and that he'd promised both to return the stuff and not to steal ever again.

"So, do you believe that Ethan's going to stop stealing?" Kurt asked.

"Yes, I really do," Emma said. "I believe he's learning to be a man of his word . . . just like someone else I know."

"You know, it's such a shame," Kurt said, leaning back on the quilt. "People like the Steins, rich people, they have so much stuff they don't even know what they have."

"Well, not all rich people are like that," Emma said.

"I don't know," Kurt said skeptically. "I see these people every summer. I spend time with their kids. And you know what? By the time the kids are eight, nine years old, they're usually spoiled rotten and totally obnoxious."

"But it's not the kids' faults!" Emma protested. "They didn't ask to be born rich. I mean, money doesn't necessarily make them bad people."

Kurt leaned over Emma and tickled her cheek with a wisp of her hair. "What's your problem?" he asked playfully. "You ready to throw me over for some rich guy on the island? Feeling a little guilty? Hmmmmm?" he teased her.

"No," Emma said stiffly, sitting up and pulling away from Kurt. "I . . . I just don't think you should stereotype people by how much money they have."

"Okay, you're right," Kurt conceded. "There are some people with money who are very cool about it, like the Hewitts. But let's get real, Emma, the Hewitts are the exception to the rule."

"You sound just like Sam," Emma said crossly.

"Do I?" Kurt said. "Well then, smart girl."

"Don't you think it's just that kind of attitude that pulls people apart?" Emma cried passionately. "You don't want to be prejudged because you're broke, do you?"

"No, but—"

"Well, then, what about 'do unto others as you would have them do unto you'?" Emma demanded.

"Whoa, whoa, time out!" Kurt exclaimed, making a *T* sign with his hands. "You don't need to get all bent out of shape over this." Kurt looked at Emma closely. "Is something bothering you?"

"No, nothing, just forget it," Emma said tersely.

"Something is bothering you," Kurt insisted, looking deeply into Emma's troubled face. He reached over and gently cupped her chin. "Emma, don't you know by now that you can trust me? I'm on your side."

To Emma's utter mortification, tears welled up in her eyes. Kurt put his arms around her and held her close.

"Shhhhh," he crooned to her. "It's okay, baby. Whatever it is, it's okay."

Emma closed her eyes, losing herself in the wonderful feeling of being safe within Kurt's arms. But all too soon Kurt moved away from her, holding her gently at arm's length so he could look at her face. "Do you want to talk about it?"

"I . . . I had a fight with Carrie and Sam," Emma admitted.

"I'm sure it'll blow over," Kurt assured her.

"Yeah, I'm just overreacting," Emma said, forcing a smile. She desperately wanted to change the subject. "You're still planning to come to the Hewitts' party tomorrow night, aren't you?" Emma asked, forcing some gaiety into her voice.

"Of course I am!" Kurt said laughing. "Why wouldn't I?"

"Well, I doubt that Carrie and Sam will be there, after our fight," Emma explained.

"You can count on me," Kurt assured her.

If only I could tell you the truth, Emma thought.

The next day Emma tried to lose herself in the party preparations so she wouldn't have to think about how mad Sam and Carrie were at her. Every time the phone rang she jumped, hoping it

170

was one of her friends calling her, but it never was.

In the afternoon Emma helped Jane and Jeff string tiny white Christmas-tree lights around the deck and in the trees in the backyard.

"Did you work things out with your friends?" Jane asked Emma when Jeff was busy on the other side of the yard.

"No," Emma sighed, wrapping the string of lights around the edge of the deck. "I mean, they haven't called me."

Jane was quiet as she ran the lights along the side of the deck. "Did you think about calling them?" Jane asked quietly.

"I guess I'm afraid to," Emma admitted.

"It might be worth a shot," Jane said. "Maybe you just need to make the first move. Go on," she urged. "Go call them now. You'll feel better."

Emma went up to her room and sat on her bed. She took three deep breaths before she picked up the phone and dialed Carrie's number.

Claudia Templeton answered the phone. Emma could hear giggling and screeching from a lot of people in the background before Claudia said hello.

"Hi, is Carrie in?" Emma asked. She was careful to sound as casual as possible.

"Stop that!" Claudia said laughing with some-one in the room. "Not you!" she added quickly into the phone. "My husband just got home and his whole band is here driving everyone crazy," she explained in a happy voice. "Just a sec, I'll get Carrie."

Emma waited a moment and then Carrie got on the phone.

"Hello?"

"Hi, Carrie, it's Emma."

"Oh, hi."

Emma could feel her pulse beating faster. She didn't know what to say. She had hoped that the tone of Carrie's voice would give her a clue.

"Carrie, I feel terrible about what happened!"

"I do, too," Carrie said.

"You do?" There was a ray of hope!

"Yes, I do," Carrie repeated. "I feel like I was lied to by someone I considered a really close friend."

"Oh, Carrie, I'm sorry," Emma whispered. "I didn't mean to! I just, just . . . I made a mistake!"

"You can say that again."

"Okay! I made a mistake! A big mistake! But I'm really sorry! Can't you forgive me?" Emma pleaded.

Carrie sighed into the phone. "I'll have to think about it some more."

"I haven't been able to think about anything else!" Emma cried. "How does Sam feel?"

"Bad," Carrie told her bluntly. "She feels like you made a fool out of her."

"Maybe I can explain—"

"I wouldn't try to say anything to her now," Carrie advised. "She's really—"

"Carrie, get off the phone, we have to order the

172

pizzas!" Emma heard someone say. Her heart sank when she realized it was Sam. "Who's on the phone?"

"Emma," Carrie told her.

"Well then, you should definitely hang up," Sam said.

"Emma? I've got to go," Carrie said into the phone.

"I understand," said Emma softly. "Have fun."

Well, so much for Jane's words of wisdom, Emma thought, as she felt the hot tears cascade down her cheeks.

"I'm wearing my party dress!" Katie cried four hours later, as Emma finished helping the little girl get ready for the big event.

"And you look beautiful in it," Emma assured her.

Once Katie was ready she went downstairs to wait and Emma ran up to her room to change. Emma pawed through her closet morosely. She didn't have a clue what she wanted to wear, what kind of an impression she wanted to make. *I'm always so worried about what people will think and I'm sick of it*, she thought viciously. On a whim she grabbed the red leather miniskirt and cropped jacket and threw them on the bed. She didn't know what impression that would make, and for once she decided not to care.

After a shower, Emma donned the red outfit, black hose, and black heels. She looked at herself in the mirror. Her perfect hair didn't go with the wild outfit. Emma threw her head upside down and brushed it from underneath. Then she sprayed it with a lot of hair spray, threw her head back, and sprayed it again. *So much for the perfect ice maiden*, she told her sexy reflection.

"Wow," was all Ethan could say when Emma came downstairs.

Jeff looked up from the CDs he was picking out over by the stereo. "I agree," he said. "Wow."

Jane came into the family room carrying a plate of cheese and crackers. She was wearing a black Lycra stretch off-the-shoulder mini dress and a single strand of pearls.

"Is it too much?" Emma asked Jane uncertainly.

"You look great," Jane assured her. "Very hot."

"Thanks," Emma said. "What can I do to help?"

"Actually, the caterers have pretty much taken over the kitchen, so there's not much to do," Jane said. "As of now you are officially off-duty," Jane added.

Emma heard the voices of the first guests arriving at the front door just as Jeff popped a Garth Brooks tape into the stereo. The rowdy music and the happy voices of arriving guests made Emma feel lower than ever. She slipped out the back door for a few minutes of solitude before party mania took over every square inch of the property.

The sun was just setting and the tiny white lights twinkled in the stillness of the backyard. Emma walked to the edge of the property and gazed out at an incredibly beautiful sunset. For just a moment of stillness she had a sense of the vastness of the world, and wondered about her place in it.

"It's all got to mean something, doesn't it?" she whispered to herself. "I don't want a meaningless life! I want . . . I want . . . I want to know what I want!"

She tried to picture herself in Africa, in the Peace Corps, doing something important. But could she really do it? Did she really want to? Or was it all just pretty words to delude herself into believing that she was different than the self-involved rich people she'd known all her life? A shiver of fear ran through Emma and she hugged herself with her arms.

"I will be different!" she whispered passionately. "I will!"

FOURTEEN

"Different than what?" asked Carrie, coming up beside Emma.

"Carrie!" Emma cried. "I'm so glad to see you! I mean, I didn't think—"

"I know," Carrie said with a small smile. "I didn't think, either. Jane told me you were out here."

"I'm just so glad you're here," Emma said fervently. "I don't suppose Sam—?"

Carrie shook her head no. "She's really, really mad, Emma. I don't know when she'll get over it."

"You mean 'if she'll get over it,' don't you?" Emma said sadly.

"I guess I do," Carrie agreed.

Emma smiled at her. "But you forgive me?"

"It's not that simple." Carrie sighed. "Let's just say that I care about you and I'm trying to keep the, um . . . lines of communication open."

"You sound like my mother's lawyer," Emma said bitterly.

"Well, what do you expect?" Carrie asked in exasperation. "God, Emma, I think you've always had it so easy you just expect that this will be easy, too!"

Emma just stood there for a second. "You're right," she said finally. "You're right."

A noisy group of revelers came out the sliding glass doors onto the patio and the music blasted out with them.

"It's getting wild in there," Carrie said.

"Wait till Jeff turns on the outdoor speakers that he hooked up," Emma said, "and it'll get wild out here, too."

"So what do you say we go get wild with them?" Carrie asked with a mischievous grin.

"Absolutely," Emma agreed.

As soon as they hit the family room which had been cleared for dancing, Howie Lawrence saw Carrie and rushed over.

"Carrie! Great!" Howie exclaimed. "I was hoping you'd be here!"

Howie had on a three-piece suit that would have been more appropriate on a forty-five-year-old CEO at a board meeting.

"Hi, Howie," Carrie said with a wry smile. "I didn't expect to see you here."

"Everybody who belongs to the club knows everyone else," Howie explained. "The Hewitts have been having this party every summer since I was a kid. Dance?" he asked hopefully.

"Sure," Carrie said. "Excuse us," Carrie said to Emma with mock formality.

"Oh, by all means," Emma responded playfully in the same tone.

There was a tap on Emma's shoulder. She turned around to see a very serious faced Ethan.

"Would you like to, um, dance?" Ethan asked.

"I'd love to," Emma answered.

She danced three fast dances with an ecstatic Ethan as the party escalated around them. Finally they stopped dancing and went to get some cider at the buffet table.

"Is this fun or what?" Wills said, coming up to them and jumping up and down. He grabbed a piece of cheese off the buffet and stuffed it into his mouth.

"Wills, you are a pig," Ethan said.

Wills shrugged and grabbed a handful of shrimp. "I'm hungry."

"Hi, Ethan," said a soft voice. It belonged to Audrey Sheppard, a very pretty girl a year older than Ethan who he knew from the club.

"Want to dance?" Audrey asked Ethan shyly.

Ethan looked over at Emma.

"Oh, it's okay," Emma assured Ethan gravely. "I'm a bit tired now."

"Stinky says that shrimp are garbage fish," Wills said, his mouth full of them. "Like they eat all the crud in the sea or something."

"Actually I don't think they're any kind of fish," Emma explained. "They're—"

Before Emma could finish, there was a hand on her shoulder.

Emma turned around and looked smack into the smiling face of her longtime, sometime, not-really boyfriend, Trent Hayden-Bishop III.

"Trent! What are you doing here??" Emma asked.

"You're surprised, right?" Trent asked gleefully.

"What are you doing here?" Emma demanded.

"I knew you'd be thrilled," said Diana, coming up next to Trent and linking her arm through his.

"Diana called and invited me," Trent explained. "I borrowed Dad's plane and flew in."

"Why, Emma!" Lorell exclaimed, joining the group, "look at you in red leather. Isn't that skirt a tad . . . skimpy?"

Emma looked at Diana and Lorell's maliciously grinning faces in shock. It had simply never occurred to her that they'd be at the Hewitts' party. *Howie was right,* Emma thought. *All the rich summer people know all the other rich summer people. What a dunce I was!*

"Poor Emma, she's in a state of shock," Trent said, hugging her.

"Yes, yes, I guess I am," Emma stammered.

"I think she's simply speechless with joy at seeing you," Diana purred.

"Come on," Trent said, grabbing Emma's hand. "I've got a surprise for you." He dragged Emma out to the yard, where he had stashed a bottle of champagne and two long-stemmed crystal glasses behind some shrubs.

"I confess, I polished off a bottle with Diana and Lorell already," Trent said. Emma believed it when he leaned near and she smelled his

180

breath. He poured them both a glass and then clinked glasses softly with Emma.

"Here's to one hell of a evening," he said, sipping the champagne.

Emma bit her lips and twirled the champagne glass nervously between her fingers. "I . . . Trent . . . I have to talk to you."

"Talk away," he said, "but have some of this first. I brought two bottles and I think we should polish them both off."

Emma took a long sip of the champagne, for courage if nothing else. "Trent, I didn't expect to see you here," she began.

"Yeah, well, I got that part of it," Trent said. "You look incredible in that outfit, by the way," he added. "I've never seen you dress like that."

"Thanks. I . . . the thing is, I have a date tonight."

Trent stopped with his glass halfway to his mouth. "A date," he repeated.

Emma nodded yes. "I didn't know you'd be here," she added lamely.

"So where is this guy?" Trent asked. "I mean, you are out here in the bushes with me," he pointed out.

"I know. I wanted to tell you alone. He's coming later, after work. Diana knew. She did this on purpose."

"Oh, come on—" said Trent.

"It's true!" Emma cried.

"How did she know?" Trent challenged Emma. "Did you tell her?"

"No, but—"

"You didn't even know Diana was going to be here," Trent said.

"She guessed that I'd be here with Kurt," Emma said.

"Kurt?" Trent asked.

"That's his name, Kurt Ackerman."

"So who is this Kurt Ackerman?" Trent asked. "He own a house on the island or something?"

"No," Emma said, "he works here. He's a swimming instructor."

Trent stared at Emma a moment. "You're kidding," he said flatly.

"No, I'm not," she said.

"You're dating a swimming instructor?"

"Yes, I'm dating a swimming instructor," Emma said flatly.

Trent laughed. "Well, here's to the egalitarian Emma Cresswell," he said, tipping his champagne glass to her. "I didn't know you had it in you."

"The truth is you don't really know very much about me at all," Emma said hotly.

"Oh, give it a rest, Emma," Trent said. "I've known you since you wore designer diapers. You're just as big a snob as Diana and you know it."

"Excuse me, I'm going in," Emma said stiffly.

"You'll forgive me if I stay out here and get blasted," Trent said. "I hate to waste good champagne."

Carrie caught up with Emma in the family room.

"Hi, I see the charming Lorell is here," Carrie said. She looked closely at Emma. "What's wrong? You look awful."

"My boyfriend is here!" Emma blurted out.

"Kurt?" Carrie asked, confused.

"No, my old boyfriend. I mean, he's not really my boyfriend, he's just someone I've dated. Not really dated, exactly . . ."

"Emma, what are you talking about?" Carrie said. "Are you two-timing Kurt?"

"No, I wouldn't do that—"

"So this is someone you broke up with?" Carrie asked.

"Not exactly—" Emma began.

Carrie just stared at Emma. "Don't you ever just tell the truth?" she asked her. Before Emma could respond, Carrie turned and walked away.

Emma snaked through the crowds of guests with no idea where she was heading. She poured herself a glass of mineral water and leaned against a wall, willing herself to breathe normally. *I'll be able to explain it all to Carrie,* Emma told herself. *Once I explain everything, she'll understand.*

"Hey," Trent said, coming up behind her.

"Hello," Emma said stiffly.

"I was a jerk," he said with a shrug.

"Yes, you were," she agreed.

"So I'm a spoiled brat. Sue me." He laughed.

"You are a spoiled brat," Emma said, but she smiled at Trent when she said it.

"Friends again?" he asked, holding out his hand to her.

"Friends," she said, shaking his hand.

"Come on, give me one dance before Aquaman shows up," Trent said, not releasing her hand.

"Trent!"

"Just kidding, just kidding," Trent said, as he led her to the dance floor.

A fast song was just ending and a slow, sexy ballad came through the sound system.

"Lucky me," Trent said, pulling Emma into his arms.

Emma couldn't very well refuse, so she moved gracefully into Trent's arms.

Trent pulled her closer. "Mmmmm, Emma in red leather. I'm seeing you in a whole new light," Trent murmured into her ear.

Now that his mouth was so close to hers, Emma could smell the champagne on his breath. It was much stronger than before. "What did you do, finish the bottle by yourself?" she asked him, pulling slightly away from the alcohol fumes.

"As a matter of fact, I did," Trent answered, dropping Emma into a dip. When he pulled Emma back up, he held her even more closely than before. Trent let his hand drift down past Emma's waist to the small of her back. He pressed slightly so that her body was molded to his.

"Trent, I think you had too much to drink," Emma began.

"Just enough, just enough," he crooned in her ear.

She tried to pull away from him again in a subtle way.

"Trent, really, stop it," she said. "You're embarrassing me."

Trent ignored her. "What do you have on under that red leather, just out of curiosity?" Trent asked, nibbling on her earlobe.

"Stop it, I don't want to make a scene!" Emma hissed at him, her face burning with embarrassment.

"You are much too well-bred to make a scene," Trent replied, letting his mouth fall to her neck.

Emma struggled away from him. "Trent, I mean it—"

A large hand hit Trent's shoulder and spun him away from Emma. It was Kurt.

"Just what the hell do you think you're doing?" Kurt demanded.

Quick as a flash, Lorell and Diana were by their sides.

"Oh, let me make the introductions," Lorell said with glee. "Trent Hayden-Bishop, this is Kurt Ackerman, swimming instructor extraordinaire. Kurt Ackerman, this is Trent Hayden-Bishop, Emma's boyfriend."

"Kurt, let's go outside," Emma urged in a low voice.

"Hey, glad to meet you!" Trent said, sticking

out his hand toward Kurt. "I hear you do a mean breaststroke!"

Lorell and Diana almost fell over laughing. Kurt looked at Emma in a state of shock.

"Kurt, please—" Emma began. She put her hand on his arm, but he shook it off.

"Really, Kurt," Lorell gasped between peals of laughter, "if you could see your face! Talk about all brawn and no brains!"

"Come outside with me, Kurt," Emma begged.

"It's just too hilarious that you bought Emma's little poverty routine," Lorell exclaimed. "The fact is, she's an heiress. Her family is—though I am loath to admit it—even richer than my family! She's been laughing behind your back since your first date!"

Emma couldn't stand the horrible pain on Kurt's face. "No, no, Kurt that isn't true."

Kurt looked at Emma. "You mean, this is all a bunch of lies?"

"It's more complicated than that," Emma began desperately.

Kurt stared hard at Emma, then he turned away from her.

"No, Kurt, please!" Emma cried, reaching for his arm.

Kurt shook her off and turned on her. "Just leave me the hell alone," he fumed and headed for the door.

FIFTEEN

Emma awoke the next morning at dawn, and all the horror of the night before came flooding back to her. It was like some horror movie stuck at the most gruesome moment, playing over and over in her mind. Emma could see the anger on Kurt's face as he left, the smug satisfaction on Lorell and Diana's faces, the hurt on Carrie's face when Emma ran past her, heading for the sanctuary of her bedroom. But really there was no sanctuary. It was all too real.

"Good morning," Jane said carefully when she came into the kitchen two hours later and found Emma sitting at the table with a cup of tea, staring out into the distance.

"Hi," Emma said quietly, taking a sip of her tea.

Jane poured herself a cup of coffee and sat opposite Emma at the table. "I gather you didn't have a great time last night," she said carefully.

"I apologize if I caused a scene," Emma said stiffly.

"Hey, what's a good party without a little scene or two," Jane said with a kind smile.

Emma covered her face with her hands. "God,

it's so humiliating," she whispered. "Everyone watching my life fall apart."

"Everyone wasn't watching," Jane corrected her.

"It felt like they were," Emma said miserably.

"Hey, Emma, want to go the club with me and Stinky?" Wills asked, running into the kitchen. He was wearing a dripping-wet bathing suit and a scuba mask.

"What have you been doing?" Jane asked him. "You're dripping all over the floor!"

"I been practicing deep-sea diving in the bathtub," Wills explained. "So do you, Emma?"

"It's Emma's day off," Jane reminded Wills.

Wills put his hands on his hips. "Mom, going swimming at the club is not work."

"Thanks for the invitation, Wills," Emma said, "but I've already made plans."

"So long, then," Wills said good-naturedly. "Trina's driving us."

"Call her Ms. Stein," Jane yelled to Wills as he tore out of the kitchen. She turned back to Emma. "Would you like some breakfast?"

"No, thank you," Emma said. "The thought of food . . ."

"I can't eat when I'm upset, either," Jane sympathized.

"Jane, I think . . . maybe I should just give you my notice," Emma whispered. She bit the inside of her lip to keep from crying. "I don't seem to be very good at any of this."

"You seem to be pretty good at feeling sorry for yourself," Jane observed.

Emma looked at Jane in shock. "How can you say that?"

Jane sighed. "Look, Emma, I'm sorry, but I could just shake you. I know something horrible happened to you, and I know you're hurting, but you have a choice. You can retreat and lick your wounds and play 'poor me,' or you can try to take some action to right all of this."

"What am I supposed to do?" Emma cried. "Sam and Carrie aren't speaking to me, Kurt despises me, Lorell and Diana have made me into the laughingstock of Sunset Island . . ."

"Would it sound like too much of a lecture if I suggested that you take some responsibility for creating this situation?" Jane asked gently.

Emma stared down at her tea. "No," she said finally. "You're right."

"Believe me, you'll feel better if you take some action," Jane said.

"Like calling Carrie?" Emma said in a small voice. "Like trying to explain?"

"That sounds like a good beginning," Jane agreed. "And Kurt?"

"I can't call him," Emma said quickly. "I never saw so much hate on anyone's face as his right before he left last night."

"He feels hurt because he cares about you," Jane observed.

"Past tense," Emma said sadly. "Cared."

Emma went up to her room and called Carrie,

but there was no answer at the Templetons'. She didn't have the nerve to try calling Sam.

Emma headed downstairs and out the door. She went down to the beach and walked aimlessly along the sand, kicking at shells and driftwood. Every part of her body hurt, as if she had the flu. *This is what it means to be heartsick*, Emma realized with tears in her eyes. *It actually, physically hurts.*

Emma walked all the way down the beach until she reached the far pier, and then started back in silence. The happy faces of the people on the beach seemed to mock her. Three young girls threw a Frisbee to each other, an elderly couple walked hand in hand in the wet sand, a little boy was being tickled by his parents as the three of them built a sand castle. Emma had never felt lonelier in her life.

As Emma approached the long, steep wooden steps that led up to the street, she thought she saw two familiar faces standing at the top of the steps. They looked remarkably like Carrie and Sam. And it was. They spotted Emma and ran down to the beach.

"Hi," Emma said carefully to her friends.

"Your nose is all red!" Carrie said. "What did you do, forget sunscreen?"

"I guess I did," Emma admitted. Carrie pulled some sunscreen out of her beach bag and handed it to Emma, then she pulled her friends into the shady area under the steps.

"You look like hell," Sam observed, plopping down in the sand.

"Thanks," Emma mumbled, drawing her knees up to her chin. "I appreciate your showing up to deliver that information."

"Hey, very good!" Sam said with a grin. "Sarcasm becomes you, it's very unladylike!"

"Sam and I had a long talk this morning," Carrie began. "I told her what happened at the party last night."

"It must have sucked," Sam said sympathetically. "Lorell and Diana are poisonous little bitches. I can't believe they set you up like that."

"It's hard to believe that anyone could get their jollies from being that cruel!" Carrie agreed.

"I sort of set myself up, really," Emma murmured.

"What does that mean?" Sam asked.

"I mean if I hadn't lied to everyone in the first place, they couldn't have done what they did," Emma admitted. "I'm just . . . I'm so sorry I lied to you both! I had this ridiculous fantasy that if no one knew about my background I could be free."

"Free from what?" Sam asked. "That's what I don't get. I mean, I would love to be rich!"

"It's hard to explain," Emma began. "All my life I've been told certain things and I've been taught to look at the world in a certain way. I was raised to believe that class was everything, that unless people had lots of money they somehow

191

weren't quite as good. I know it sounds horrible, but when you're a kid you just don't know any different than what your parents tell you. . . ."

"Right," Carrie agreed. "Kids believe what their parents tell them. I guess racist parents raise racist kids, for example—which is a frightening thought."

Emma nodded. "But as I got older, I started to see things differently. The things that were important to them became less and less important to me, like material things, like judging people by their class and religion . . . it's sickening!" Emma cried fervently.

"So have you told your parents how you feel?" Carrie asked Emma.

"I've tried to," Emma began, "but . . ." She stopped and took a deep breath. "No, that isn't true. I haven't tried to because I know they'd never, ever understand. My mother is an heiress, and my father has spent his whole life overachieving to prove to the world that he didn't marry her for her money. Neither one of them ever spent any time with me. My dad just tries to buy me things to make up for it. And my mother can only concentrate on me for five minutes before the subject turns back to her."

"That's terrible!" Sam said. "And you don't have any brothers or sisters?"

Emma laughed bitterly. "Well, in a way. My mother is so scared to death of growing old that she constantly tries to pretend she's my sister."

"And she's really engaged to Austin Payne?" Carrie asked, wide-eyed.

"It's true," Emma admitted. "I never in the world expected to see him on Sunset Island. After I saw him fooling around with about ten different women, I called my mom to warn her. She said I was just jealous. She's planning to show up on the island, for Austin's opening. Of course she told me that before she hung up on me."

Sam pushed her red curls out of her eyes. "God, Emma . . . I don't know what to say."

"Say you don't hate me," Emma pleaded.

"Oh, Emma, of course I don't hate you!" Sam leaned over and hugged Emma. "Of course Carrie is a much tougher customer . . ."

Carrie smiled at Emma. "We're your friends, you nut."

Relief flooded through Emma and she grinned at her friends. "Thanks," she said simply.

"What are you going to do about Kurt?" Sam asked.

"Now there's someone who really hates me," Emma said sadly, "so what is there to do?"

"Well jeez-Louise, you give up easily!" Sam said. "I thought you were crazy about him!"

"I feel like I have a hole in my heart," Emma said sadly. "I know Kurt. He really hates lying. He'll never listen to me."

"Never say never!" Carrie instructed.

"Come on," Sam said, standing up and brushing

the sand off her legs, "let's go back to the house and you can get your purse and we'll go to the Play Café and figure out a strategy for you."

Emma's phone rang just as the girls reached the third floor.

"Hello?" Emma answered breathlessly.

"Hi."

It was Kurt! He was calling her! Emma sat down on the bed and gripped the phone tightly.

"Hi, Kurt." Carrie and Sam plopped down on the rug.

"About last night," Kurt said, "I shouldn't have just run out like that," he said gruffly.

"I . . . I wanted to explain. I still do," Emma said hopefully.

"Okay," Kurt agreed. "I'm willing to listen. I'm not the kind of guy who judges someone without letting them tell their side."

"I really can explain!" Emma said eagerly. "I'm just . . . I'm so glad you called!"

"I have to drive the hack tonight until ten," Kurt said, "but I thought maybe I could come pick you up after that, about eleven?"

"Fine, great," Emma said. "See you then."

Emma looked at Carrie and Sam, and then all three of them started jumping up and down and screaming.

"He called me! He called me!" Emma screamed. "I'm going to see him tonight!"

"I knew you weren't giving him enough credit!" Carrie crowed triumphantly.

194

"What are you going to wear?" Sam demanded.

"God, I don't know," Emma laughed. "I haven't even thought about it yet."

"A trench coat with nothing underneath would probably get big results," Sam said innocently.

Emma threw a pillow at Sam as the phone rang again.

"Hello?" Emma said, with laughter in her voice.

"Well, don't you sound cheerful, dear." It was Kat.

"Hello, Mother."

"I'm on your little island, at a place called the Sunset Inn," Kat said. "The room service here is atrocious, by the way. I want you to know I feel terrible about our fight, Emma. You know I can't stand discord."

"I wasn't lying to you about Austin, Mother," Emma said firmly.

"Oh, please, Emma," Kat said irritably. "Austin is here with me right this minute. He's totally thrilled that I came in for his opening. Shall I put him on the phone so he can tell you himself?"

"Don't bother," Emma said.

"Look, Emma, I did not call to fight with you. Can't we be friends?" Kat pleaded. "After all, best girlfriends don't fight over guys, now do they?" she added playfully.

Emma resisted the urge to scream.

"Here's what I'd like to do," Kat continued.

"The gallery opening is at seven o'clock, cocktails at six. The party after the opening will be here at the hotel, in the Edwardian Room. How about if you meet Austin and me at, say, six-thirtyish for cocktails, and then we'll all go to the party together."

"I have plans, Mother," Emma said in a steely voice. "I'm going out with my friends."

"Are they presentable?" Kat asked gaily.

"Of course they're presentable! What kind of a question is that?" Emma demanded.

"Well, then, they will be my guests for the evening," Kat said regally. "Do remember that it's black tie, darling."

"She drives me nuts!" Emma screamed after she hung up the phone. She threw herself down on the bed.

"I take it your mom is here?" Carrie asked.

"Not only is she here, staying in what is undoubtedly the most expensive suite at the Sunset Inn—with, I might add, that slime-bomb she's engaged to—she wants me to bring you both to the private cocktail party before the opening, and to the private party afterwards at the inn."

"What about your seeing Kurt?" Carrie asked.

"I could do both," Emma admitted. "But listen, you two really do not have to do this."

"Are you kidding?" Sam exclaimed. "Only the most megarich of the megarich on this island are invited to that party! It'll be a blast!"

Carrie shrugged. "It'll be okay. I'll bring my camera and take pictures."

Emma smiled at her friends. "You two are really great."

Sam stretched and lifted her hair from the back of her neck with an expansive sigh. "She only says that because it's true."

SIXTEEN

Emma stared at her reflection in the mirror and faced a moment of high anxiety. She had chosen the dressiest yet most sedate outfit that she'd purchased at the Cheap Boutique, a black raw silk suit with a very slim, very short skirt. Yet the idea of facing her mother in something so "cheap and off the rack"—at least from her mother's point of view—made Emma feel self-conscious and ill groomed.

This is ridiculous, Emma said to herself, as she brushed her hair and tied it back with a black velvet ribbon. She realized she was trying to compensate for the outfit by making sure her hair and makeup were exactly as her mother would expect—perfect and understated. Then she got so irritated at her own insecurity that she rebelliously pulled on a pair of textured black stockings and slid her feet into black open-toed pumps with a high, narrow heel.

The three girls had agreed to meet in front of the Play Café so they could walk over to the gallery together. Sam had borrowed a car and picked Carrie up. They were already waiting when Emma walked over from the Hewitts'.

"You look incredible!" Carrie exclaimed when she saw Emma.

"Really?" Emma asked anxiously. "I wasn't sure about the hose and shoes."

"Are you kidding?" Sam asked with a laugh. "That's what makes the outfit. It says ladylike from the neck down, and hussy from the feet up."

"Schizophrenic dressing!" Carrie laughed, too. "I think it could catch on!"

"You two look quite fabulous yourselves," Emma told them. Carrie had on an oversized loose-weave pink sweater over a long, flowing gauze-and-chiffon flower-print skirt. When the oversized sweater slipped off one shoulder Emma could see the narrow strap of a lacy pink leotard. Sam looked stunning in a sheer antique white lace blouse and a black and white polka-dot lace miniskirt.

"We are rather gorgeous," Sam decided. "We should get someone to take our picture."

Just at that moment a van pulled up to the Play Café. Out jumped Billy, Pres, and the rest of the guys in Flirting with Danger.

"Ah, opportunity has reared its lovely head!" Sam said with a grin.

Billy went around to open the back of the van and caught sight of the girls out of the corner of his eye.

"Hi there!" he called to them, and started walking over.

Sam quickly pulled Carrie's sweater off one shoulder and then shot Carrie an innocent look.

"It's Carrie, right?" Billy said, pointing a finger at her.

"Right," Carrie answered happily.

Billy looked at Emma and Sam. "Sorry, I'm terrible with names."

"Emma and Sam," Sam filled in.

"You're playing at the Play Café tonight?" Carrie asked Billy.

He nodded. "Isn't that why you're here?"

"We're going to the art gallery opening," Sam said, cocking her head in the direction of the gallery across the street.

"Ah, a woman of culture," Pres drawled, coming up. "Very intriguing."

"Too bad," Billy said, looking at Carrie, "I was hoping we could talk some more, you know, between sets."

"You two can go hear them play," Emma said quickly. "I can go over to the gallery by myself."

"No way," Carrie said firmly.

"Ditto," said Sam.

Emma smiled at them gratefully. Maybe Bill and Pres had no idea what Emma was facing at the gallery, but Carrie and Sam did.

They got Billy to take a picture of the three of them with Carrie's camera before they said their good-byes and headed across the street to the gallery.

"This is great," Sam told Carrie. "Believe me, guys in bands are used to having girls fall all over them. We'll be much more attractive to them if we act like we're not interested."

Carrie laughed. "You should write a book. *The Samantha Bridges Book on Getting Guys.*"

"Hey, it isn't easy being a vixen," Sam said seriously.

Emma was only half-listening, anxious as she was about seeing her mother and Austin. Amidst the well-dressed crowd in the gallery, Emma spied Kat and Austin in the main room, holding champagne glasses and chatting with another couple.

"Over here, darling!" Kat waved gaily to Emma.

Emma caught the flicker of disapproval on her mother's perfectly made-up face when she saw Emma's outfit.

"Sweetheart!" Kat exclaimed, kissing the air on either side of Emma's head.

"Hello, Mother," Emma said. "These are my friends, Carolyn Alden and Samantha Bridges. Hello Austin," she added in a hollow tone.

"Please call me Carrie," Carrie said with a friendly smile.

"And I'm Sam," Sam added.

"Call me Kat!" Emma's mother said gaily. She turned to Austin, who was standing next to her in an impeccably cut tuxedo. "This is my fiancé, Austin Payne." Kat linked arms with Austin and sipped the glass of champagne she held in her other hand.

"Hello," Austin said with a smile. "I believe we met when I was hanging my paintings the other day."

"Yes, I believe we did," Sam answered sweetly.

"This is Buffy and Randall Arpell," Kat added, introducing the couple they had been chatting with.

"Charmed," Buffy said. "Your mother is looking radiant, Emma. Why, she looks as if she could be your sister!"

"Isn't that sweet of you to say," Kat murmured, snuggling serenely against Austin's bicep.

"Won't you excuse us?" Emma said. "We'd like to go look at the paintings."

When the girls got on the other side of the room, Emma exploded. "I cannot stand it. He's so disgusting! The whole thing is disgusting!"

"He is your basic toad," Sam agreed.

"Totally phony," Carrie added.

Emma grabbed a glass of champagne off the tray of a passing waiter and drank it down quickly.

"Whoa!" said Carrie. "That's not going to help."

"Believe me, seeing Austin Payne through a blur helps."

The girls wandered through the gallery, studiously avoiding Kat and Austin until it was time to leave for the party at the inn. Carrie took a lot of pictures. People assumed she was from the press and kept posing for her.

"I don't want them to pose!" Carrie said to her friends in frustration. "I want candids."

"Believe me," Emma said dryly, "these people are always posing."

"Why don't you girls come in our limo," Kat suggested on the way out of the gallery. "The Arpells have their own car, so we've plenty of room."

"Great!" Sam answered quickly. "I've never been in a limo!"

The uniformed driver held the door as they climbed into the back of the sleek car. Austin poured everyone champagne from the bar and turned on the stereo system.

"Wow, this is great!" Sam exclaimed happily. "I feel like I'm in a movie or something!"

Austin smiled appreciatively at Sam's exuberance. Kat put her hand on his thigh possessively. "Isn't she sweet, Austin?"

Emma stared out the window and tried to ignore the whole thing. *It has nothing to do with me*, she told herself. *Soon this will be over and I'll be back with Kurt and I can just live my own life.*

The minutes at the party crawled by for Emma. Sam was having a great time, flirting and dancing with handsome guys in perfectly cut tuxedos. Carrie wandered around taking photos and trying to escape from Howie Lawrence, who seemed to show up everywhere she went. Emma sat in a darkened corner, sipping a glass of mineral water. She couldn't wait until it would be time to go meet Kurt.

"Emma, sweetheart, are you feeling all right?" Her mother stood by her side, the ever-present glass of champagne in her hand.

"Yes, I'm fine."

"You're not being very social, if you don't mind my saying so," Kat chided.

"I'm not feeling very social," Emma answered.

Kat sat down next to Emma. "What is this new petulance you seem to have developed? I feel like you're going to bite my head off all the time!"

Emma sighed. "I'm sorry."

"I know what it is," Kat said slyly. "You don't want me stealing your thunder."

"That is not true," Emma began.

"Isn't it?" Kat said coolly. "Look at the outfit you chose to wear. I've never seen you in a skirt that short. And those hose and those shoes!"

"I happen to like this outfit," Emma said through clenched teeth.

"Fine," said Kat, holding up a hand. "I refuse to argue with you. I'm too happy. Not to mention the teeniest bit tipsy," she added confidentially. "Come with me to the little girl's room."

Kat took Emma by the hand and led her to the ladies' room. "I'm having such a fun time!" Kat chirped gaily through the door to the stall. She came out and washed her hands in the pink porcelain sink. A uniformed woman handed Kat a small pink towel to dry her hands.

"I love the way Austin looks in a tuxedo, he's so dramatic!" Kat said to Emma dreamily, handing the used towel to the bathroom attendant without a glance. Kat studied her face in the mirror and frowned slightly, then pulled the edges of her face gently towards her hairline. "Do you think I need a face-lift?"

"No, you look great," Emma said honestly.

Kat opened her evening bag and dropped a dollar bill in the tray for the bathroom attendant, then she pulled out her lipstick and began reapplying it. "A lot of people think I've had one, including Buffy Arpell," Kat said. "I told her it's good genes, good diet, staying out of the sun, and of course, being in love helps." Kat blotted her lips and dropped the tube back in her bag. "Ready to go?" she asked Emma.

"Sure," said Emma.

Kat snapped her evening bag shut and looked at her daughter with concern. "Are you okay, Emma? I wish you'd talk to me."

"About what?" Emma asked.

"The things mothers and daughters talk about!" Kat said with exasperation. "Are you having fun here? Do you like your job? Are you dating anyone?"

"Yes to all three," Emma said.

Kat's eyebrows shot up in surprise. "You're dating someone? Who is he?"

"You wouldn't find it interesting, Mother."

"Of course I would!" Kat said in a hurt tone of voice. "Why must you always underestimate me?" Kat took Emma's hands and sat her down on the pink satin-covered stools that lined the wall. "I'd love to hear about him," she said eagerly.

"Well," Emma began shyly, "his name is Kurt. He's very handsome."

Kat nodded encouragingly.

"I like him a lot," Emma continued. "He's a very special person, very honest and sincere."

"Kat, darling, there you are!" Buffy exclaimed as she whooshed into the ladies' room. "I just saw Austin with some nymphette in a white dress that is barely decent," she confided, pulling a comb out of her evening bag. "If only we were young enough to get away with that, eh, Kat?"

Kat stood up quickly and squeezed Emma's hands. "We'll talk later, darling," she promised, then scurried out of the ladies' room.

Emma looked at Buffy's self-satisfied face in the mirror. *I've got to get some air*, she thought, and headed for the front porch of the inn.

The first thing she saw was Austin leaning against a pillar, staring up at the full moon, smoking a cigarette. Before she could turn around to avoid him, she saw a gorgeous girl in a skintight white dress come around the corner of the inn.

"There you are," the girl said softly, walking over to Austin. "I've been looking for you everywhere."

The girl snaked her arms around Austin's neck and gave him a long and passionate kiss. "I've been wanting to do that all night," she purred huskily, rubbing her body against his.

"Jeez, not here!" Austin whispered. He grabbed the girl's hand and they moved quickly into the shadows.

Emma turned away in disgust and practically rammed into her mother. The look on Kat's face told Emma that Kat had seen everything.

"Mother, I—"

"Don't," Kat said in a shaky voice. "Don't say a word." She smoothed her hair with a trembling hand. "I seem to have developed a terrible headache," she said to Emma. "Do express my regrets to your friends." With that she turned and walked regally toward the bank of elevators, her head held high.

"Maybe I do underestimate her sometimes at that," Emma murmured to herself, watching her mother's retreating figure.

"Where have you been?" Sam asked Emma breathlessly when they ran into each other in the lobby. Sam held her hair up off her neck and fanned herself.

"Around," Emma said vaguely. She wasn't ready to tell anyone about what had just happened with her mother.

"I have been dancing with this incredible guy!" Sam exclaimed. "He's Dutch or Swedish or something—one of those Nordic countries. Anyway, he owns, like, dozens of art galleries all over the world. He said I should be a model!"

"What an original line," Emma replied, laughing.

"Maybe I really should think about it." Sam shrugged. "It beats working for a living!"

Carrie spied her friends in the lobby on her way to the ladies' room. "Help! Save me from

Howie! He keeps talking about all these bands his dad works with because he thinks it will impress me, and I've never heard of any of them!"

"Sorry, I can't save you because I have to go meet Kurt," Emma said happily. "I can't wait!"

"Maybe we could sneak over to the Play Café and listen to Billy's band?" Carrie asked Sam hopefully.

"I'd have to leave Lars, who is rolling in money, to go play groupie to Pres, who is undoubtedly poor as a church mouse," Sam sighed.

"Take it from me," Emma said. "Money does not make the man."

"I do have a certain weakness for the way Pres fills out a black T-shirt," Sam admitted.

"Listen, thanks for coming to this thing with me," Emma told her friends.

"Call me tomorrow and tell me every detail of what happens with Kurt," Sam ordered.

"Me, too!" Carrie said.

"Such voyeurs!" Emma laughed and headed back to the Hewitts'.

As soon as Kurt's car pulled·in the driveway, Emma raced out. She couldn't wait to see him.

"Hi," she said softly, smiling at him in the dark.

He smiled at her and backed his car out of the driveway.

"Are we going to our spot?" Emma asked eagerly.

"The dunes? That's as good a place as any," Kurt said.

They didn't talk until they had pulled over to

the side of the road at the dunes. They got out of the car and then leaned against it, staring up at the clear night sky.

Kurt folded his arms. "If you want to talk, I'm ready to listen," he said finally.

Emma stared down at her hands. "I don't know where to begin."

"How about name, rank, and serial number? I mean, I don't have any idea if anything I thought I knew about you is true," Kurt said.

"Most of it is true!" Emma said. "How I feel is true."

"Let's deal with the lies, then," Kurt said.

"Look, I . . . I never told you about my being rich. At first it just didn't seem important. And then as I got to know you, I thought you wouldn't like me anymore if you knew," Emma confessed.

"Go on," Kurt said.

"I wanted to tell you the truth, so many times! But every time I'd start to tell you, you'd go off about how spoiled and obnoxious rich kids were. How could I tell you I was one of them?"

"So it was, like, convenient? That's why you lied?" Kurt asked, bewildered.

"I told you, I thought you wouldn't want to go out with me if you knew," Emma explained. "And I didn't really lie to you, Kurt, I just didn't tell you. It's hardly the same thing."

Kurt was quiet for a moment, staring at Emma. "You are such a hypocrite," he said finally.

"I'm not!"

Kurt laughed an ugly laugh. "You are unbelievable. All that crap you gave me about how concerned you were about Ethan learning to be honest, and you're a bigger liar than an eleven year old kid!"

"No, don't say that—," Emma began.

"And what about the guy that was all over you at the party? You told me you broke up with your old boyfriend! I suppose you've got some *convenient* explanation about him, too."

"I've dated him, but—"

"Damn, I must be the biggest fool of all time!" Kurt yelled, slamming his hand down hard on his car.

"He's not my boyfriend!" Emma yelled. "I've never felt about anyone the way I feel about you! He was drunk, that's all."

"So what was he doing at the party if he isn't your boyfriend?" Kurt challenged her.

"Diana invited him!" Emma cried. "She did it on purpose because she hates me. I had no idea he'd be there. Look, Kurt, it's true that I've dated him. And I'm sorry, I should have told you that I didn't have a chance to tell him about us. But I never really thought of him as my boyfriend! I've known him for years. But we've never been . . . intimate or anything like that." Emma was trying desperately not to cry.

"You expect me to believe that?" Kurt yelled. "You looked pretty intimate at that party, Emma, so cut the innocent act."

"It's not an act!" Emma protested. "I've never—"

"Please, just save it," Kurt said with disgust. "For all I care right now, you could have hopped from bed to bed with every rich playboy on this island."

"I'm not like that!" Emma screamed. She was really crying now, great sobs bursting from her chest. "Please, Kurt—"

"Stop crying," Kurt ordered gruffly. He opened the car door and reached for the box of tissues on the dashboard and thrust it at Emma.

"Thank you," she mumbled, blowing her nose. "I'm really sorry, Kurt. I was wrong. But you don't know what it's like. You come from this great family, where everyone loves each other. You were raised with a real sense of . . . values about life. My mother's concept of value is how far up the social ladder a person is."

"Poor little Emma," Kurt said sarcastically. He shook his head. "You are really something. Am I supposed to feel sorry for you because you were born rich?"

"No, but you could try listening to me instead of just judging me," Emma replied. "The truth is, I hate my life! I—"

"You hate your life?" Kurt asked incredulously. "God, you amaze me! You are the most self-involved person I've ever met! You know nothing about real life. I'm killing myself to put myself through school. My sister couldn't get a new dress for graduation because we didn't have the money. I've watched good, honest, hard-working people on this island who were forced to move away from the homes they love because they couldn't make a living here anymore. That's my life, Emma. That's what's real to me. Not the snivelings of a poor little rich girl."

"Well, who died and made you God?" Emma whispered.

Kurt shook his head. "Forget it, Emma. We have nothing to talk about." He walked around to the driver's side of his car and got in.

"Fine," Emma said, getting in the car and slamming the door shut. Kurt's attitude stung her.

Kurt started up the car and they drove in silence back to the Hewitts'. Kurt stopped the car in the driveway.

Emma turned to him. "Please Kurt, if you'd just listen to me."

"Listen to what, Emma? More lies? More twisting the truth because it suits you?"

"I'm not like that!" Emma protested.

"You're exactly like that." He reached over Emma's lap and opened her door.

"I don't want to leave like this!" Emma cried.

"I don't really care how you leave, Emma, just as long as you do it."

Emma tried to stifle the sob that came to her throat as she ran into the house.

"This can't be happening, this can't be happening!" she whispered over and over to herself. But all she could hear was Kurt's hard, cold voice as he opened the car door for her. *"I don't really care how you leave, Emma, just as long as you do it."*

SEVENTEEN

Emma woke up the next morning with her eyes red rimmed and swollen from crying. She reached over and picked up her journal, which she'd written in compulsively the night before as she cried over the pages.

I can't believe how much this hurts. I had the hugest fight with Kurt. It was so scary and he was so cold. I was a fool to fall for him. Love is terrible! If you fall in love you give the other person too much power over you. I guess my mother and I aren't so different after all. Everyone turns into a fool when they fall in love . . .

The phone rang and Emma answered it.

"Hello?" she croaked. Her voice sounded hoarse from crying.

"Do you have a cold, Emma?" It was Kat.

"No, I'm fine," Emma said, not sounding fine at all.

"I'm leaving in a couple of hours, and I'd like to have brunch with you before I go," Kat said.

"I really have a terrible headache, Mother," Emma said.

"Brunch will do you a world of good," Kat instructed.

"I really don't feel up to it, Mother."

Silence. "I see," Kat said finally. "Well, I certainly can't force you to have brunch with me if you don't want to."

The hurt in Kat's voice tugged at Emma. She could resist the imperiousness, get angry at the foolishness, but she fell for the hurt every time.

"Mother? Wait, I'm sorry. Of course I'd love to see you before you go. Brunch is fine."

"You're sure you want to?" Kat asked.

"Sure I'm sure," Emma said. "I'll be there in forty-five minutes."

Emma forced herself to get up, shower, and get dressed. She made it over to the Sunset Inn in under an hour.

"You look terrible," Kat said when Emma sat down opposite her at the Sunset Inn restaurant.

"Maybe I'm coming down with something," Emma murmured. She opened the menu to hide her face from her mother.

"I'll have poached eggs on whole-wheat toast, orange juice, and herbal tea," Kat ordered.

"The same," Emma said. She knew she'd never be able to eat a bite of it.

"I'm thrilled to get out of this hotel suite, I can tell you that," Kat said, sipping her water. "Do you know they didn't even turn down the bed?"

"Maybe that's because Austin was still in it,"

Emma said, regretting the words even as they left her mouth. "I'm sorry. That was an awful thing to say."

"Yes, it was," Kat said quietly.

The waiter brought them their tea in a small silver pot, and Kat poured them both cups.

"Do you get so much satisfaction over having been right about him?" Kat asked Emma.

"I don't get any satisfaction at all," Emma told her truthfully. "But it really hurt me when you didn't believe me, when you just hung up on me. I'm not a liar!" Even as Emma said this, Kurt's opinion of her rang in her ears. She was so a liar. She just picked and chose her own lies. Tears came to Emma's eyes, and she blinked them back.

"Emma, what is it?" Kat asked, reaching across the table for her daughter's hand.

"Nothing," Emma said, but to her embarrassment she couldn't stop the tears from running down her cheeks.

"Emma, whatever is the matter?" Kat asked, with real concern in her voice.

"Well, you know the guy I've been seeing. I . . . I think I'm in love with him," Emma cried, "and he broke up with me last night. He hates me!"

"Oh, Emma, I'm so sorry," Kat said.

Emma pulled a tissue out of her purse. "I know I'm making a scene, I'm sorry," Emma said with a sniffle.

"Don't worry about that now," Kat said. "Why do you think this boy hates you?"

"He just does," Emma said, unwilling to tell her mother the truth. She looked at her mother with tear-filled eyes. "It hurts so much to love someone and not have them love you back!" she whispered.

Tears came to Kat's eyes as she stared at her daughter across the table. "Yes, Emma, I know the feeling," she said quietly. "Well," Kat said, trying to laugh, "aren't we a pair? I have to stop this or I'll have raccoon eyes."

The waiter brought their eggs and set them on the table.

"Take them away," Kat said imperiously to the waiter.

"Is something wrong?" the waiter asked in confusion.

"We just don't want them," Kat said. "I expect to be charged for them, of course."

"Yes, madam."

"You should have been born to royalty," Emma said to her mother, laughing and wiping away her tears.

"So, what do you do now?" Kat asked her daughter.

Emma shrugged. "What do you do now?" she countered.

"Well, the engagement's off," Kat said. "I wouldn't even let Austin in the suite last night. He begged," she added with obvious satisfaction.

"So you're not going to see him anymore?" Emma asked hopefully.

"As I said, the engagement is off. You don't necessarily throw everything away because of one tiny indiscretion," Kat went on.

"Mother, the girl at the party last night is a different girl than the one I saw him with before," Emma said.

Kat sipped her tea. "You're very young, Emma. You have a very simple way of looking at the world. The fact of the matter is that Austin makes me happier than your father ever did."

"Mother, I really don't want to hear this," Emma said.

Kat fiddled with the diamond-and-pearl bracelet that Austin had given her. "As I said, Emma, you are still very young. Say, I have a marvelous idea!" Kat said, changing the subject. "I'm on my way to the Golden Chalet in Gstaad for a month of rest and relaxation," Kat announced, naming the most expensive, most exclusive health spa in the world. "Why don't you come with me! Wouldn't that be fun?"

"I can't just pick up and come with you!" Emma said. "I have a job! I have responsibilities!"

"Really, darling, I think we both know that life at the Howells' will not stop if you leave."

"Hewitts'," Emma corrected.

"Whatever," Kat said. "Besides, I know men. If you want this boy back, leave him for a while, act as if you don't care a fig about him. Then when you come back, all thin and fit and glowing, he'll be panting for you!"

Emma stared at her mother. *She's not talking about me at all,* she realized. *She's talking about herself.*

Kat laughed a brittle laugh. "I know men, dear. Believe me, I know men."

Emma stared at her mother's perfect face and felt unutterably sad. "Excuse me, Mother, I have to get back," she said. "Thanks for the invitation, but I'm going to stick this out." Emma pushed back her chair and stood up.

"You can stay a little longer," Kat coaxed.

"No, I really can't," Emma told her. "I have to work this afternoon. It was nice to see you." She kissed her mother's cheek and headed for the door.

In a daze Emma returned to the Hewitts'. A terrible thought kept going around in her head: *What if I'm just like my mother?*

"Oh Emma, am I glad to see you," Jeff said when Emma walked in the door. "We arranged a private swimming lesson for Katie. Jane had to go into Portland, and I've got tons of work I need to finish on a brief. Could you take her over to the club?"

"Of course," Emma said, trying to keep her voice from quivering. Going to the club meant seeing Kurt, which was the last thing in the world she wanted to do. Jane had obviously kept what she knew about Emma's personal life a secret. Jeff had no idea how desperately she did not want to see Kurt.

"Hey, Emma, this swimming lesson is going to be only me," Katie chirped to Emma in the car. "And Sally," she added hastily.

"Won't that be fun," Emma said automatically.

Emma parked the car and took Katie's hand to walk her over to the junior pool. Kurt was standing near the pool talking to Ginny. He laughed at something she said, then caught sight of Emma. He deliberately turned his back on her and continued his conversation.

Emma settled in a chair as far away from Kurt as possible. "Okay, Katie," Emma said, "go on over there for your lesson."

"Sally's going to try swimming today," Katie said in a little voice.

"She is?" Emma said. "Well, that's wonderful!"

The little girl rubbed Sally's matted hair across her arm and looked up at Emma from under her lashes. "Could you please sit close by me?" she asked. "Sally is a little scared."

Emma knelt down and hugged Katie. "Of course I'll sit close to you," Emma assured the little girl. Hand in hand they walked over to the pool. Emma took the seat closest to the shallow steps leading into the water.

"Hello, Katie!" Kurt said to the little girl with an encouraging smile. He pointedly ignored Emma.

Emma felt as if her heart would break. To be so

close to him and watch his cold, closed-off face was like some terrible torture.

"Are you ready to try getting in the water?" Kurt asked Katie.

"Sally first," Katie decided, thrusting her doll at Kurt.

"Good idea," Kurt agreed gravely.

With Katie watching from the edge of the pool, Kurt took the doll and walked her down the steps and into the water.

"I think she likes it," Kurt said to Katie. "What do you think?"

"She thinks it's wet," Katie answered seriously.

Kurt held his hands under the doll and let it float on its back. "She's a very good swimmer!" Kurt told Katie. He held out his hand to her. She hesitated a moment, looking over at Emma. Emma gave her a nod and an encouraging smile. Slowly Katie walked over to Kurt's outstretched hand and took her first steps into the water. She walked down one step, then another, then another. And then Kurt gently put his hands under her arms and lifted her so that she floated on the water.

"Emma! Look at me! I'm swimming!" Katie cried, splashing her arms.

"I see! You're wonderful!" Emma called to the little girl. For the briefest of moments she caught Kurt's eye, both of them grinning from ear to ear with happiness for Katie. Kurt quickly looked away. Emma pretended she had something terribly important to get from her purse, so that

Kurt wouldn't see the quick tears that came to her eyes.

After Katie's lesson, Ethan and Wills showed up at the club with Stinky Stein. Katie went to the afternoon play group, where they had planned activities for preschoolers. Emma found a chaise lounge by the pool. She slathered sunscreen on herself, lay down, and closed her eyes. Exhausted from the night before, she quickly fell asleep.

She woke up when she felt Wills's damp hand on her arm an hour later.

"Hey, Emma, do you have any money? I want to play video games with Ethan and Stinky."

"Sure," Emma told him groggily, reaching for her purse.

The boys wanted to stay until Trina came for them, so Emma collected Katie and drove home.

"I swimmed!" Katie screamed to her father when they walked in the door.

"That's great!" Jeff said, swooping the little girl up in his arms. "Mommy will be so happy to hear that!"

"What?" said Jane, who was just walking in the front door.

"I swimmed!" Katie repeated.

"She really did," Emma confirmed. "She was wonderful."

"Oh sweetie, I'm so proud of you!" Jane said, putting her arms around her husband and her little girl. Jeff kissed Katie, then he kissed his wife.

223

Emma gulped down the anguish she felt watch ing them. Jane and Jeff loved each other an their kids so much. It was obvious to anyone wh saw them. Emma started slowly up the stair thinking that no one had ever loved her that wa; wondering if anyone ever would.

"Emma! Your friends are here!" Etha screamed up the stairs.

Emma was startled awake and looked at th clock by her bed. She'd been asleep for thre hours!

"Hi!" said Sam, as she and Carrie came in Emma's bedroom. "Leading a life of leisure, see."

"Wow, I really fell out," Emma said, rubbin her face sleepily.

"Listen, I've got great news!" Carrie sai "Graham Perry is playing a concert on the islan next week, at the civic center. It's a fund-rais for the new public park they want to build or past the dunes," Carrie explained. "Anywa; guess who has backstage passes?"

Emma laughed. "Let me see . . ." she por dered. "Could it be . . . you?"

"Yes!" Carrie said with glee. "And you an Sam, too! Graham said I could have three! And can bring my camera and take pictures bacl stage! I might even be able to sell them t *Rolling Stone* or something!"

"Down girl, down!" Sam said, patting Carrie

shoulder. "She's a tad excited," Sam said, flopping down on the window seat.

"Wait, it gets even better," Carrie continued. "Guess who the opening act is? Flirting with Danger!"

"I think our little Carrie has a crush on a certain extremely cute lead singer named Billy," Sam said.

"Well, not a crush," Carrie said. "I mean, I hardly know him. He seems . . . nice."

"You lie like a rug!" Sam laughed. "Admit it, you want to jump his bones."

"He does have very cute bones," Carrie admitted with a grin. "I think he only likes me as a friend, though. I'm not exactly his type."

"How do you know?" Sam demanded.

Carrie shrugged. "You know what I mean. You saw the girls at the Play Café last night, the ones that were all over him. They were really sexy, and they had on those micro-miniskirts, and tons of makeup, and they had really big hair and really big—"

"Egos," Sam filled in. "They also have really small minds."

"Maybe, maybe not," Carrie said.

"Well, my opinion is he likes you a lot," Sam said loyally. "He came over and talked to you on almost every one of his breaks, didn't he?" she pointed out.

Carrie nodded yes happily.

"I'm happy for you," Emma told Carrie sincerely.

Carrie noticed the lack of enthusiasm in Emma's voice. "Oh, I'm sorry, Emma," she said, sitting down on the bed. "I know you're upset about Kurt. I wasn't thinking."

"How did you know?" Emma asked her. "When I left you two last night to go meet him, I thought everything was going to turn out fine," she said bitterly.

"We ran into him at the Play Café this afternoon," Sam explained.

"You did?" Emma asked, her heart pounding in her chest. "Did he ask about me? Did you talk to him?" she asked anxiously.

"Yeah," Sam said. "The boy was bummed."

"He hates me," Emma said tearfully.

"No, he doesn't," Carrie said. "He was angry, I admit, but he couldn't stop talking about you."

"I tried to explain everything to him, I really did!" Emma said earnestly. "But he wouldn't listen. Nothing I said made any difference. He had this attitude that was like a brick wall."

"I hope you don't mind that we did this," Sam began tentatively, "but we told him some of the things that you told us—about your mother and everything."

"It's okay," Emma said with a sigh.

"He seemed to listen," Carrie told her. "Maybe it was easier hearing it from a third party."

Emma hugged her knees to her chest. "I hope so," she said sadly. "But I don't hear the phone ringing off the hook."

"Finally I told him he was acting like a jerk,

Sam said. "I told him you deserved another chance, and if he wasn't willing to give it to you then he was idiot."

"Sam is not one to mince words," Carrie said with a smile.

"I appreciate your trying," Emma told her friends, "but I think it's all over between us. I just wish it didn't hurt this much." Emma stood up and went into the bathroom to wash her face. "God, what a day."

After dinner, Emma felt so full of restless energy she decided to go for a jog on the beach. She changed quickly into her sweats and ran down the steps to the sand. After some quick stretches she jogged easily along the hardened sand where the water met the beach. The air was crisp and cool, and the night shone with a million stars. Emma felt tiny and insignificant, and lonelier than ever.

Finally, exhausted, she jogged back to the Hewitts' and took a long, hot shower. She kept hoping the telephone would ring, but it never did. Finally she fell into a deep and dreamless sleep.

Thwack!

Emma thought she heard a strange sound and struggled up from her sleep. She decided it was nothing, so she turned over and fell back into her dream.

Thwack! Thwack!

This time she opened her eyes and listened

carefully. She really had heard a noise. She'd heard it more than once.

Thwack! Louder this time. It seemed to be coming from the window. Emma climbed out of bed and kneeled on the window seat, peering out into the dark backyard.

Thwack! She jumped back as a stone hit the glass window. So that's what it was! She opened the window carefully and poked her head out.

"Hi!" Kurt called up in a whisper.

"What are you doing?" Emma whispered.

"Throwing rocks at your window."

"I can see that," Emma said. "I mean, why?"

"I thought it was too late to call. I didn't want to wake you," Kurt whispered.

I must be dreaming this, Emma said to herself, *because that makes no sense at all.*

"Can you come down?" Kurt asked.

Emma pulled on jeans and a T-shirt and ran downstairs. *Please don't let this be a repeat of last time*, Emma prayed.

"You forgot your shoes," Kurt said when he saw her. He stared at her a moment. "Emma, I'm sorry. I was a jerk."

Emma was afraid to believe him. "I thought you never wanted to see me again," she said carefully.

Kurt ran his hand through his hair. "I guess I kind of have a temper. It's not one of my finer qualities," he admitted. "I ran into Sam and Carrie this afternoon," he added.

"They told me." Emma shivered in the night air.

"You need to get your bare feet off the grass," Kurt said. He lifted her easily and sat her on the redwood picnic table, then he sat down next to her.

"At first I couldn't hear a word they said," Kurt admitted, looking down at his hands. "It just sounded like more excuses, but . . . I couldn't stop talking about you," he said sheepishly. "I couldn't stop thinking about you. Finally Sam hauled off and told me what an idiot I was." He grinned. "I'd hate to get on that girl's bad side."

"I didn't ask them to defend me, you know," Emma said quickly. "It wasn't my idea."

"I know that," Kurt said. "Anyway, after I left the café, I went to drive the hack for a few hours. I mean, I still wasn't convinced, but I couldn't stop thinking about you, seeing your face in my mind. . . . So I get a call for a pickup at the Sunset Inn, going to the ferry. The dispatcher told me the customer's name was Mrs. Cresswell."

"My mother?" Emma asked in shock.

Kurt nodded. "Carrie and Sam told me she was on the island. I have to admit I was curious to meet her. She had no idea who I was. So I pick her up, and the first thing she does is order me to put her suitcases in the backseat because she thinks the trunk is dirty. Then she complains the air-conditioner in the taxi is broken. When I open the window for her she screams that it's ruining her hair."

"That's my mother," Emma said wryly.

"Finally I get the air-conditioning working again," Kurt continued, "so she calms down. She does this whole number about some health spa she's going to. She tells me how she lives this very healthy life-style, which keeps her young and fit. I'm just listening, you know? Just kind of nodding now and then. Finally she asks me in this very coquettish voice how old I think she is. I say I have no idea. She never does tell me how old she is, she just leans forward so I can feel how firm her bicep is. Then she studies my face, and tells me I have a face of a movie star. Then she asks me why I'm wasting such good looks behind the wheel of a taxi, but before I can answer her she's complaining about how horrid the Sunset Inn is. Finally, we're at the ferry. I unload her luggage and she just sits there, waiting for me to open the door for her, as if I were her chauffeur. When I finally do open the door, she complains that the skirt of her suit has gotten dirty from the taxi. She did tip me well, though," Kurt added.

"She was nervous," Emma said. "She and her fiancé had a fight." To Emma's surprise, she found herself defending her mother.

"I didn't tell you all this to bitch about your mom," Kurt said. "Believe me, I've had all kinds in my taxi. It's just that meeting her, hearing her, I suddenly got a picture of what it must be like for you. She's the most insecure woman I've ever met in my life."

Emma shrugged.

"The point is, Emma, you were right," Kurt said earnestly. He picked up her hand and held it. "I was judging you. I still don't think what you did was right, but at least I think I can kind of understand why you did it."

"Really?" Emma asked in a small voice.

"Really," Kurt said.

"I know I was wrong," Emma said. "I mean, you were right about some things, even though I didn't want to admit it. But Kurt, the way I feel about you . . . that was never a lie!" Emma whispered fervently.

Kurt turned to her and stroked her cheek with the back of his hand. "Do we get to try again?"

"I will if you will," Emma said.

As an answer, Kurt took her in his arms and kissed her until all the stars in the sky seemed to be dancing in her head.

"Hey!" cried a tiny voice from above. Kurt and Emma looked up to see Katie, peering out her bedroom window.

"Hey, yourself!" Kurt called up happily.

"How come you were kissing Emma?" Katie asked.

"Because I love her!" Kurt said.

"That's a good reason," Katie decided.

"It's a very good reason," Emma whispered, smiling at Kurt. And then nothing else existed but Kurt, the stars, and a night that Emma wished would never end.

Meet . . .

JENNIFER

by Melanie Friedman

She's the girl who's ready for anything! Especially if it's
new, outrageous, and fun. Meet Willi—a perfectly normal
girl whose life would be normal too—if only her best friend
Jennifer wasn't absolutely crazy!

__#1 WHAT'S NEXT, JENNIFER? 0-425-12603-X/$2.75

When Jennifer cooks up a plan to go get Willi a date with
Robbie Wilton for the Halloween dance, her scheme back-
fires. Willi thinks that Robbie has fallen for Jennifer instead.
Is this the end of Willi and Jennifer's friendship?

__#2 NO WAY, JENNIFER! 0-425-12604-9/$2.75

Will anyone at Wellbie High still read the school newspaper's
advice column, "Dear Heart," when they find out it's written
by a lowly freshman? Willi writes the column and is trying to
keep that a secret. But Jennifer has decided that "Dear
Heart" should come out of hiding, and Willi can't stop her!

__#3 YOU'RE CRAZY, JENNIFER! 0-425-12605-6/$2.95

Jennifer's dad seems to be getting serious with the
mother of her archrival. Will Jennifer and Tessa end up as
step-sisters? Not if Jennifer can help it! She and Tessa
bury the hatchet long enough to set up a scheme so
diabolical that Willi just wants to hide until it's done!